This spelling contest is nerve-wracking,
Joe thought, as he watched another
member of his team bite the dust.

"Okay, Joe," Mr. Pruitt said. "Your word is
synagogue."

Joe spelled out the word.

"That is incorrect," Mr. Pruitt announced gently.

Joe looked at Sam, then went to his desk.

As Sam moved up to the "hot seat" at the head
of the line, the dismissal bell rang. The students at
their desks started gathering up their backpacks
and other belongings.

"Hold it, hold it," Mr. Pruitt called. "The
spelling bee is not over."

Joe and the other students looked at him.

"Each team now has two members remaining,"
he said. "We'll finish this contest tomorrow."

Sam and Amanda
moved past each other as
they went to get their
books.

"Good job, Amanda,"
Sam said.

"Yeah," Amanda said.
She raised her chin in a ges-
ture of challenge. "I guess
tomorrow we'll find out in
front of the whole class
who the best speller is."

The Adventures of WISHBONE™

Ivanhound

by Nancy Holder
Based on the teleplay by Darla Opava
Inspired by *Ivanhoe*
by Sir Walter Scott
WISHBONE™ created by Rick Duffield

Big Red Chair Books™, *A Division of* **Lyrick Publishing**™

This book is a work of fiction. The characters, incidents, and dialogues are products of the author's imagination and are not to be construed as real. Any resemblance to actual events or persons, living or dead, is entirely coincidental.

 Big Red Chair Books™, *A Division of Lyrick Publishing*™
300 E. Bethany Drive, Allen, Texas 75002

Edited by Pam Pollack

Copy edited by Jonathon Brodman

Continuity editing by Grace Gantt

Cover concept and design by Lyle Miller

Interior illustrations by Don Punchatz

Wishbone photograph by Carol Kaelson

Library of Congress Catalog Card Number: 99-63425

ISBN: 1-57064-431-4

First printing: January 2000

10 9 8 7 6 5 4 3 2 1

*This book is for Pastor Sue
and the congregation of
Mission Hills United Methodist Church.*

FROM THE BIG RED CHAIR . . .

Oh . . . hi! Wishbone here. You caught me right in the middle of some of my favorite things—books. Let me welcome you to THE ADVENTURES OF WISHBONE. In each of these books, I have adventures with my friends in Oakdale and imagine myself as a character in one of the greatest stories of all time. This story takes place in the late fall, when Joe is twelve, and he and his friends are in the sixth grade—during the first season of my television show.

In *IVANHOUND*, I imagine I'm Ivanhoe, a noble and brave knight from Sir Walter Scott's *IVANHOE*. I return home from a war far away and find my country full of danger and in a state of chaos. This medieval tale is about courageous warriors facing evil knights, betrayal between brothers, life-threatening jousting tournaments, and damsels in distress.

You're in for a real treat, so pull up a chair, grab a snack, and sink your teeth into *IVANHOUND!*

CHAPTER ONE

Twelve-year-old, brown-haired Joe Talbot and his classmates at Sequoyah Middle School were bent over their spelling-test papers. Finally, their English teacher, Mr. Pruitt, closed his book. He sat at his desk and looked around the room at his students.

He said, "Time. Pass your test papers forward, please."

Joe and the other kids did as their teacher asked. On the other side of the room from Joe, Amanda Hollings sat at the head of her row. She wore a calm expression. It was clear to Joe that she had finished the test early. Spelling was definitely a breeze for her—just the way digging in Joe's neighbor's yard was such a breeze for his Jack Russell terrier, Wishbone.

At the thought of the little white dog with brown and black spots, Joe grinned. If Joe knew

Wishbone, he was waiting right outside school for the bell to ring. He would be ready for an afternoon of fun and adventure.

"Amanda," Mr. Pruitt said, "would you collect the tests for me?"

Amanda picked up her row's stack of tests. Then she moved to the next row. Finally, she reached the row that included Joe's two best friends, Samantha Kepler and David Barnes. At the head of the row, Sam—as her close friends called her—put down her pencil. But David kept writing. He frowned, looking very serious. As Joe watched, Amanda waited in front of Sam for the papers.

Sam quietly cleared her throat. David jerked his head up. He laid down his pencil and took the tests passed from behind him. Adding his own paper, he handed the stack to Sam. He flashed a little smile at Amanda.

Joe's row came next. Then Amanda handed all the tests to Mr. Pruitt.

"Thank you, Amanda," the teacher said. As Amanda returned to her seat, Mr. Pruitt rose. "Now, here's your assignment for tomorrow. I want all of you to practice your spelling. We're going to have a class spelling bee."

Joe joined the chorus of lighthearted moans and groans.

Mr. Pruitt said, "Please, pay attention." With a finger held in the air, he made an imaginary line down the center of the room. "This half of the room will be Team A."

That was Joe's half. He was glad to see that Sam and David would be on his team. So was a very good speller named Robin.

"This half will be Team B." That was Amanda's side of the classroom. "I want each team to select a captain who best represents your group."

Joe looked at his team members. *Should it be Robin?* he thought. *How about David? Maybe Sam . . .*

Amanda raised her hand. She asked eagerly, "Will this spelling bee count as part of our grade?"

Mr. Pruitt shook his head. "No," he said. "This assignment, besides being about spelling, is all about teamwork and the spirit of competition."

The bell rang. Joe grabbed his books and then he stood up.

Over the chatter of the students leaving the room, Mr. Pruitt called out, "Now, remember, team captains must be chosen before class tomorrow."

"Not Joe, not Joe, not Joe," Wishbone said, as student after student rushed out of the school building. The Jack Russell terrier sniffed hard at each pair of pants, each shoe. He wagged his white tail with anticipation.

Then . . . *woo-cha!* He caught sight of Joe's blue

jeans and brown-plaid shirt. Wishbone's sensitive black nose had picked up the familiar scent of his best friend, Joe Talbot.

"Joe!" he barked in greeting.

Joe headed toward the bike rack with his other best friends, Sam and David. Sam wore a blue-plaid shirt and jeans. She liked wearing a baseball cap, which she turned backward. David's jeans and gray-and-white-striped shirt were neatly pressed.

"Hey, what's up, buddy?" Wishbone said happily. He leaped up from his resting place and trotted to catch up with the kids. "Hey, pal!"

Joe, David, and Sam stopped at a bench next to the bike rack. Wishbone jumped onto the bench so that his friends wouldn't have to lean down too far to pet him. The three gave him a few friendly pats and scratches.

Then Amanda Hollings and a few other students from Joe's class walked over. One of them was Nathaniel Bobelesky. He and Wishbone had shared a few adventures together.

Wishbone wondered if anyone had a snack for him tucked inside one of their backpacks. He sniffed around. Amanda raised her chin and smiled confidently at Joe and his friends.

"Do you think you'll be ready for the contest?" she said.

Contest? . . . What contest? Wishbone cocked his head at Sam.

Sam smiled back at Amanda and asked, "Who did you pick as your team captain?"

Nathaniel Bobelesky said, "Our best speller, Amanda."

Amanda looked pleased and proud.

Wishbone wasn't sure what Amanda was going to be the captain *of.* But he knew she had a strong personality and that she would be a good leader. Just like a certain dog he knew . . .

"Who did you choose?" Amanda asked Joe.

Settling back on his haunches, Wishbone waited for Joe's answer.

Joe didn't answer right away. "Uh . . . we haven't decided yet."

So the position had yet to be filled. That was really good news, especially for an eager, young—and attractive—dog who was always on the prowl for new challenges. *I'd love to be a team captain,* Wishbone thought. *So how about picking me?*

Wishbone put on his most captainlike pose, his muzzle held high.

Amanda grinned at the kids. She said, "Well, I'm sure you can find *somebody* on your team who can spell well." She began to walk past Sam. Then she paused shoulder to shoulder beside her and said, "Good luck, Samantha."

All right! Wishbone pawed the air with excitement. *Teams and contests and captains!* The situation reminded him of a wonderful tale packed with adventure—and burning castles, and kings and knights in disguise, and even Robin Hood!

"So, a challenge has been set before us, a contest of courage and strength!" Wishbone exclaimed to Joe and his friends. "Just like the first tournament in *Ivanhoe.*"

They weren't listening to him. Wishbone sighed impatiently. Nobody ever listened to the dog.

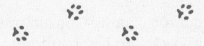

Ivanhoe was written by Sir Walter Scott. The book was published in 1819. It was set in medieval England during the 1100s. It's the story of a young knight's homecoming after fighting in the Crusades—a terrible war in a faraway land. The brave warrior Ivanhoe returns to find

England deeply divided between the Normans and the Saxons.

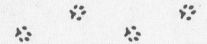

Yes! Wishbone's imagination started galloping away with him. In his mind, he was traveling back to a time of romance, derring-do, and danger. He imagined he was the noble Saxon warrior Wilfred of Ivanhoe.

CHAPTER TWO

As seagulls circled overhead, Ivanhoe's heart beat with joy. His wooden boat neared land. The salty scent of the air filled his nose. He had finally come home to England, the country of his birth. He had been gone for many years.

He leaped from the boat. His four paws splashed in the chilly seawater. Beneath his heavy black woolen cloak, his chain-mail armor—flexible battle gear made of metal rings linked together—clanked.

As he trotted onto the sandy shore, he raised his muzzle to look at the darkening sky. Thunder rumbled in the gathering clouds. A bad storm was brewing.

With a heavy heart, he thought of another stormy night from long ago. His tail drooped at the painful memory. It was the night his father had turned against him. Unlike his boat, Ivanhoe had no safe harbor. He no longer had a home or a loving family. In all the world, he stood alone.

Ivanhoe's father was named Cedric the Saxon. Their home was a large estate called Rotherwood. Moss and twisting vines grew on the low stone walls surrounding the property. A thick mat of grass, called thatch, was used as the roof covering. The moat, a large, wide ditch that was filled with water, surrounded the castle and kept out invaders. Rotherwood was like a small island. It was a sea of calm, protected from dangers beyond.

That terrible night years ago, Ivanhoe had walked back and forth in the great banquet hall. The huge room was smoky and warm from the cooking fire after the night's great feast. Piles of logs in the two huge fireplaces glowed.

Then at last, Ivanhoe's love, the lady Rowena, appeared. She ran to him. The lady leaned forward and wrapped her arms around his neck.

"Oh, Ivanhoe," she whispered. "I came as soon as I got your message."

"I did not think that you would come," he murmured.

"How could I stay away?" She reached out her hand to scratch between his ears. On trembling paws, he backed out of reach.

She is not for me, he thought sadly.

Rowena was the most beautiful Saxon maiden in England. Her hair gleamed like the summer sun that warmed his fur on a lazy afternoon. And her eyes were as blue as the ocean.

Because she had no parents, Rowena lived at Rotherwood. She had been placed under Cedric's care. She owed him loyalty—her complete loyalty. And Cedric had commanded her to marry a young Saxon nobleman named Athelstane.

Ivanhoe knew Rowena had to obey Cedric. He was glad that he had to leave home for war before the wedding. He couldn't stand to see her marry another.

"I must leave at dawn to join the king's army." With his right front paw, he touched his sword. Soon he would fight in a faraway land. "Forget me, my lady, and marry Athelstane."

"But it is you I love, Ivanhoe," Rowena said to the knight. Her blue eyes filled with tears. "I will love you forever."

"And I love you. But our love goes against my father's wishes." He pawed the air as if to touch her, but he dared not. "You must obey him."

"I cannot marry Athelstane. I do not care for him." She gazed into Ivanhoe's dark brown eyes. "I will wait for your return."

Ivanhoe shook his head. "It is very likely that I will die in battle far away. You may never know that I'm dead. You will wait uselessly. And you may die a lonely old woman."

Rowena began to cry bitterly. "But why must you go?"

"King Richard is my sworn leader. And he has commanded me," Ivanhoe replied. "I must do as he says. And you must do what my father says."

"No." She put her lovely delicate hands to his face, cupping his muzzle. "I don't love Athelstane. I love *you*."

From the sleeve of her sea-green gown, she pulled a bright red scarf of the finest silk. On it was an "R," for Rowena, woven in gold thread.

"Wear this always," she said, "and think of me."

She wrapped the scarf around his neck. Ivanhoe bowed over his forepaws. Then he said, "You are too kind, my lady. I don't deserve such an honor."

"That's the truth! You don't deserve it!"

Ivanhoe's father, Cedric, stepped from the shadows. He was furious. His bushy blond eyebrows met at the bridge of his nose. His long blond hair trailed over his powerful shoulders. His fists were clenched. His cloak of fur-trimmed red velvet swirled like a wild wind as he moved.

"You are one ungrateful lad!" Cedric shouted at Ivanhoe. "You know that Rowena must marry Athelstane. And yet you dare to claim her heart!"

Ivanhoe was ashamed. He hung his head as a sign of obedience.

"No, my father," he said. "I do not claim her heart. In fact, I am going to leave Rotherwood in the morning."

"What?" Cedric took a step backward. "You are leaving? Why?"

"King Richard has ordered me to fight with him in the Crusades," Ivanhoe replied.

Wishbone here. The Crusades was a two-hundred-year war between the Christians and Moslems. It began in the year 1100. Christian soldiers all over Europe were on a religious mission to free the Holy Land, Jerusalem, from the Moslems. Jerusalem is now located in modern-day Israel. Now, back to our story.

"What madness is this?" Cedric cried. "We have spoken about this many times already. I thought you understood my orders."

"Father," Ivanhoe pleaded, heartsick to hear

Cedric's angry tone. "In all other things, I am yours to command."

"You cannot disobey your father about anything!" Cedric thundered. "And I forbid you to go!"

"My king has commanded me to join him."

Cedric shook his head angrily. "He is not your king. King Richard the Lion-Hearted is the king of the Norman people. You are a Saxon." Cedric's face was red from shouting at his son. "No son of mine will obey a Norman's commands!"

One hundred years before Ivanhoe was born, England was ruled by a Saxon king. Then a group of warriors called Normans sailed from their homeland in France and invaded England. They killed the Saxon king and put their own ruler in place. From then on, all the kings of England were Normans.

My great-grandfather fought the Normans, Ivanhoe thought. *When the Saxons lost, my family did not give up their anger. My own father still keeps the old hatred alive.*

Ivanhoe raised a paw. "King Richard has finally united the Normans and the Saxons in peace. We are one English people."

"Never!" Cedric raised his strong arms and shook his fists. Then he slammed his hands down on the long wooden banquet table. "We will never be one people!"

Ivanhoe sighed. His ears and tail drooped. It

was no use. He and his father would never see eye to eye as long as they lived.

Ivanhoe's belief about being one united people was not shared by many others. Most Saxons wanted a Saxon king to rule once more. Many of them supported Cedric in his fight.

Athelstane, Rowena's intended husband, was the last living Saxon of noble blood. Rowena also had an excellent Saxon pedigree. Cedric dreamed of making them king and queen of England. Most Saxons would gladly die to make that dream come true. For that reason, the Normans hated Cedric.

"I have spent my entire life serving our people," Cedric declared. "I raised you to be proud of your Saxon blood. I made you into a warrior. As a knight, you must stand up for our family's honor."

Ivanhoe raised himself tall on his four legs. "I have always followed the rules of knightly conduct. I am a fierce warrior, and I have always honored the code of chivalry. As a knight, I have been true to my word to honor my king, respect women, be brave in battle, aid the helpless, and fight injustice."

Cedric ignored Ivanhoe's words. "It is my order that you turn your back on Richard. If you do not, I will turn my back on *you*."

"But, Father, I am your son," Ivanhoe said.

"Do you serve Richard the Norman?" Cedric asked Ivanhoe.

Ivanhoe bowed over his forepaws. "Yes, Father. I do serve and honor him."

"Then you are my son no longer." Cedric pointed to the large wooden doors at the entrance of Rotherwood. His hand shook with fury. "Leave here—and never come back. You are a stranger to my heart. You are a stranger to me!"

"No! Please, don't do this," Rowena begged Cedric.

Silently, Ivanhoe raised his muzzle. He walked slowly to the large doors. An iron ring hung down on one of them. Grimly, he opened the doors. Then, without looking back, he stepped out of the warmth into the violent storm.

The freezing rain poured down in buckets. Lightning flashed over the muddy courtyard of the gray-stone castle. As Ivanhoe tramped through the mud, a thousand memories flooded through his mind. There, when he was young, he had chased squirrels with the castle children. In one corner, his father had taught him how to handle a sword. Cedric had carved for him his very first wooden sword.

Ivanhoe's eyes closed against tears. His heart ached. Stiff and silent, he splashed through the mud. He passed a hundred places he had marked as his territory. His sharp nose could smell the dozens of bones he had buried in the gardens. They had all come from the mouth-watering feasts at Cedric's generous table.

Every memory I have is of this place, he thought. *I am now an outcast, with no name. I have nothing but my honor.*

Over the crashing noise of the storm, he heard his lost Rowena cry out his name. "Ivanhoe, I shall always love you!"

While the thunder continued to crack, Cedric bellowed, "Silence, girl! As far as I am concerned, Ivanhoe is dead!"

I have no family. I am alone. I am as good as dead, Father, Ivanhoe thought.

Ivanhoe shook off the memories of the time gone by. He stood on the sandy, moonlit beach. His tail drooped with sadness at his painful thoughts. He was older now, but no wiser. He still loved Rowena against his father's wishes. He still served Richard the Lion-Hearted, his Norman king. And he longed for his father's forgiveness.

In the darkness, someone cried, "Help us! Save us from the Normans, or we are dead!"

"Who calls for help?" Ivanhoe shouted. "I am a knight, sworn to protect the weak!"

Cast in yellow moonlight, two young boys in coarsely woven clothing ran toward him. They were both very thin. Their eyes seemed huge. The older one carried a small chunk of bread in his right hand.

A soldier in heavy armor ran behind the boys. He swung a sword over his head and cried, "Halt, you Saxon thieves!"

"Halt yourself!" Ivanhoe commanded. He planted his four paws firmly in the sand, ready for battle. "Why are you chasing young children?"

The soldier frowned at him. "Who are you to question me? I am a Norman soldier, loyal to Prince John. These two miserable Saxons stole bread from the village baker!"

"That's not true, sir," said the younger boy. "The baker gave it to us, because we're starving."

"It's because of the Normans that we're forced to starve," added the older boy. "They have taken all of our money."

"Hold your tongue!" the soldier ordered. He pointed at the boys with his sword. "Those who speak badly of Prince John must die!"

"Whoa! Whoa! Whoa!" Ivanhoe said. "Who is this Prince John?"

The boys and the soldier all stared at Ivanhoe in surprise.

"Where have you been?" the soldier demanded. "Prince John is the ruler of all England."

"I have been in Jerusalem," Ivanhoe answered. "With King Richard. And, as I recall, *he* is the ruler of all England."

"That used to be so, sir knight," said the older boy. "But Richard has been gone so long that his brother has taken over. Prince John, that is. He lets the Normans do whatever they want to do. And the Normans treat us Saxons like dogs."

23

"That's terrible," Ivanhoe said.

"That's the way it is," the soldier said. "King Richard is not here. But Prince John is. And all good Englishmen do what he orders."

"Well, *I* am an Englishman. And I do *not* follow his commands," Ivanhoe said bravely.

"Then prepare to die!" the soldier cried.

Without warning, he attacked Ivanhoe with his heavy steel sword. Ivanhoe growled and pulled his sword from its scabbard.

The courageous knight was an excellent fighter. He dodged the soldier's thrust with ease. Then Ivanhoe lunged. He carefully aimed his own weapon at the man.

The soldier dropped his sword and fell to his knees. "I surrender," he said, clasping his hands in fear. "Kill me not, good sir knight."

"I will give you your life," Ivanhoe said, "if you will swear that you will harm no more Saxons."

The man frowned. "But Prince John orders us to harass them and make their lives miserable."

Ivanhoe was puzzled. What had happened while he had been away at war? It seemed England was being torn in two.

"Well, for your information, *I* happen to be a Saxon." Ivanhoe pointed his sword at the man's chest. "So, do you promise to be nice?"

The man bowed his head. "I do so promise."

"Very well. Go in peace."

The soldier bowed nervously, then hurried away.

The younger boy said to Ivanhoe, "There's to be a grand jousting tournament. If you went, I'm sure you would win the day. Prince John himself will be there."

"Where will this tournament be held?" Ivanhoe asked. "And when?"

"At Ashby-de-la-Zouche, in six days," the boy answered.

"Hmm . . . I will think on it," Ivanhoe told him. "I do love a contest."

But first he would go to Rotherwood. He wanted to make sure that Rowena and Cedric were safe. The Normans had hated his father for years. With Prince John in charge, Cedric might well be in danger.

I will go in disguise, Ivanhoe decided. *My father has forbidden me to cross his path. I will make sure he does not recognize me.*

The clouds broke and rain drenched Ivanhoe. Within seconds, his fur was soaked. It was not a good night for man or beast to be out.

It didn't matter. He must get to the castle as soon as possible.

I have come home from one war only to fight another, Ivanhoe thought. *Perhaps it is my fate to die in battle, after all. But I care not, if my death buys life for my father and my beloved.*

Ivanhoe was unafraid of what the future might hold. He was a knight. He would face any contest with bravery and honor.

Surrounded by the violent storm, he raced for Rotherwood.

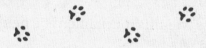

Wow! Ivanhoe is one brave guy. And so are some friends of mine. Let's see what's happening to Sir Joe, Sir David, and Lady Sam!

CHAPTER THREE

love a contest, Wishbone thought, as he jumped off the school bench.

After teasing Joe and his friends, Amanda and Team B confidently walked away. The dog and the rest of the pack . . . er, Team A, watched.

"Who are we going to pick as our captain?" Sam asked.

Eagerly, Wishbone did a flip. "Oh, me!" He wagged his tail. "I'm a born leader. Fearless, dashing, bold." He raised himself up onto his hind legs. "Handsome and furry."

No one seemed to notice his go-getter spirit. The group was lost in thought.

"A spelling bee. Team captain . . ." Joe said.

"A spelling bee," Wishbone repeated. He was no longer quite so eager about being the leader. "I think you guys are just the people for the job. Yes, sir, uh-huh."

Robin said, "I nominate David."

"Or David," Wishbone said helpfully. "David's good."

"Me?" David was startled at the suggestion. "No. Not me," he said firmly. "Maybe a math quiz, sure, lay it on me. But spelling?" He made a face and shook his head.

The team looked frustrated.

Then David said, "I think Sam should be our team captain."

"Yeah," Joe agreed, his spirits brightening.

"You're always reading," David reminded her.

Sam shrugged modestly.

"Sam is perfect," Robin declared. "All in favor of Sam as our team captain, say 'aye.'"

Everyone said "aye."

Sam looked both pleased and a little uncertain.

"Motion passed." Joe grinned at her. "Don't worry. We'll beat 'em."

"Sure we will," David agreed, nodding.

"It's not 'them' that I'm worried about," Sam admitted. "It's 'her.'"

Wishbone nodded to himself. *She means Amanda,* he thought. *I'm worried about her, too. She can spell as well as I can dig.*

The next day in school, Sam headed up Team A. David, Joe, and the other members of the team stood nervously next to her. On the other side of the classroom, Amanda and her teammates seemed to be ready for the contest to begin.

Mr. Pruitt said, "Welcome to the first round of the spelling bee. If you misspell the word given to you, you will be disqualified and return to your seat. The team with the last remaining member to spell all the words correctly will be the winner."

Joe and the others nodded to show that they understood the contest rules.

Holding the spelling book in his hand, Mr. Pruitt then added, "Teams, are you ready?" All the students nodded. He opened the little blue book. "Let us begin. Team A, your first word: *bulletin.*"

Sam closed her eyes with relief.

Good, she knows it, Joe thought.

"Bu-ll-et-in," Sam spelled.

"Correct," Mr. Pruitt announced.

David glanced happily at Sam, then waved a fist at Joe.

Sam went to the back of the line. David was up next for Team A.

Mr. Pruitt said to Amanda, over on Team B, *"Sibling."*

She raised her chin. *"Sibling,"* she repeated back to him. "Sib-ling. *Sibling.*"

"Very good." Mr. Pruitt sounded pleased by the way the contest was going.

Next it was David's turn. Nervously, he folded his arms across his chest.

"Collage," Mr. Pruitt said.

"Collage. Co-ll-age," David spelled hopefully.

"Correct." Mr. Pruitt turned to Team B, where Nathaniel Bobelesky was up. *"Jewel."*

"J-e-w-el?" Nathaniel tried, raising his brows.

"Yes!" Mr. Pruitt was delighted.

Joe thought, *So far so good.* Then he stepped up to the front of Team A.

"Immediate." Mr. Pruitt pronounced the word carefully.

"Immediate. Imm-e-d-iate."

"Very good," Mr. Pruitt said.

Joe looked happily at Robin as she stepped up to the front of the line. Now he would be off the hook for a while.

The contest continued. The words got harder, and the contestants started dropping like f-l-i-e-s. Sometimes Mr. Pruitt chuckled at a misspelling. Then at other times he put on a sad face or murmured softly, "Sorry."

"*Orchestra.*"

"*Ridiculous.*"

"*Mandatory.*"

Robin made a mistake in spelling a word. She returned to her seat.

"*Reservoir.*"

Another member of Team B had to sit down.

"*Exquisite.*"

A member of Team A bit the dust.

This is nerve-wracking, Joe thought.

Amanda rolled her eyes and stared at the ceiling when one of her teammates misspelled *xylophone*.

The competition heated up. Everyone in the room was feeling the tension.

"Okay, Joe," Mr. Pruitt said. "Your next word is *synagogue.*"

Joe took a deep breath. "*Synagogue.*" He closed his eyes for a second, concentrating. "S-y-n- . . ." He began again. "S-y-n-a . . ." Again, he hesitated. "Syn-a-g . . ." He said quietly to himself, "*Gogue . . .*" Then he said to Mr. Pruitt, "G-o-g-e."

"I'm sorry, but that is incorrect," Mr. Pruitt announced gently.

Joe looked at Sam, then went to his desk.

As Sam moved up to the "hot seat" at the head of the line, the dismissal bell rang. The students at their desks started gathering up their backpacks and other belongings.

"Hold it, hold it, everyone" Mr. Pruitt called. "The spelling bee is not over."

Joe and the other students looked at him.

"Each team now has two members remaining," he said. "We'll finish this contest tomorrow."

Sam and Amanda moved past each other as they went to get their books.

"Good job, Amanda," Sam said pleasantly, as she passed by the girl.

"Yeah," Amanda replied. She raised her chin in a sign of challenge. "I guess tomorrow we'll find out in front of the whole class who the best speller is."

"Guess we will," Sam answered, gazing back at Amanda.

So Sam and Amanda are ready for the big joust . . . er, I mean the high point of the class's spelling bee.

Ivanhoe is plenty busy himself. Most knights can't read or write. But they sure know how to do a lot of fighting! So let's see what Ivanhoe is up to. Turn ye p-a-g-e!

CHAPTER FOUR

For four days and nights, Ivanhoe walked through thick English forests. He passed hundreds of trees. There was a variety of wide-branched oaks, beeches, and hollies. Moss-covered trees tempted him to make a pit stop. The forest floor was covered with gnarled tree roots, acorns, and prickly bushes.

Now and then he splashed through a marshy swamp. Then he made his way through rich, grassy forest glades. The fragrant countryside made his heart swell and his tail wag. This was the England he had longed for while fighting so far away in Jerusalem. The land near his home was filled with nature's bounty.

But England was also filled with Norman violence against the Saxon people. As Ivanhoe hurried to Rotherwood, he would stop long enough to right some of the wrongs he saw around him. He gave a poor old woman on the road the last of his supply of bread and cheese.

"Blessings on you, young man," the old woman said. "How are you called, that I might thank you properly?"

Ivanhoe said to the woman, "I am but a lowly traveler, and I have no name."

Finally, reaching the edge of a thick forest, he knew he was almost home. He raised his muzzle to inspect the darkening sky. Another storm was about to rain down upon him.

His sharp sense of hearing picked up a rumble that sounded like thunder. It was a group of men on horseback. They galloped toward him. He put his paw to the sword hidden beneath his cloak.

Standing proud and brave like the purebred he was, Ivanhoe faced the strangers. They surrounded him on their large, sturdy war horses. The men were dressed in full battle gear, like knights. But over their armor, fine silks and satins gleamed in the fading light. Ivanhoe saw that their heavy cloaks were made of fur and fine wool.

They are very rich and powerful men. They must be Normans, Ivanhoe realized.

Their leader's dark eyes blazed as he stared down at Ivanhoe. His black moustache and dark hair added to his look of evil. But Ivanhoe was not afraid at all of the powerful-looking older warrior. He was afraid of no man.

"Who are you?" the knight demanded. The wind caused his hair to whip around his face.

"Only a lone traveler," Ivanhoe replied, keeping his voice calm and even.

"By your roughly woven clothes, I take you for a lowly Saxon, as well," the knight said rudely. "Therefore, you must serve us. My Norman warriors and I require food and rest this night. Tell us where we might find them."

The fur all along Ivanhoe's back rose at the knight's insulting tone. He quickly covered a growl by clearing his throat.

"I'm on my way to Rotherwood. It is the castle of Cedric the Saxon. Like all Saxons, he keeps the custom of hospitality. Any traveler may stop there to ask for food and shelter . . . *ask politely,*" he added under his breath. The Norman did not hear him.

"We require a guide. Take us there at once," the knight ordered him.

Ivanhoe bowed stiffly over his forepaws and replied, "As you wish." He would deal with these rude Normans at a later time. He wanted to get to Rotherwood as soon as possible.

Just then, thunder drummed and lightning split the sky. Icy torrents of rain pounded one and all, both Norman and Saxon. Ivanhoe's clothes and fur were instantly soaked. He was glad to have on the cloak and hat he wore as a disguise. They gave him some protection from the pouring rain.

The storm raged. Ivanhoe led the ungrateful travelers to the main gates of Rotherwood. His heart pounded. He kept his head low.

No one must know who I am, Ivanhoe said to himself. *I am breaking my father's command never to return. But I must know that he is safe,* Ivanhoe told himself. *And Rowena, as well. But now she is married to Athelstane.*

The very thought made his tail droop. It nearly dipped into the mud.

The powerful-looking knight with the wild, dark eyes blew on his hunting horn. He cried out impatiently, "Open the gates at once! We demand shelter for the night!"

Slowly, the heavy wooden drawbridge lowered over the moat. Ivanhoe pulled his wide-brimmed hat low over his face. The group rode over the bridge and splashed through the mud in the courtyard. Ivanhoe's heart pounded as they neared the castle entrance.

I have not seen my father in many years, he thought. *Yet, the memory of his face I have carried with me always. And I still wear Rowena's scarf. She claims my heart to this day.*

A servant led the travelers inside to the great banquet hall. Ivanhoe's muddy paws padded softly on the earthen floor. To him, every footstep boomed like the beating of a great drum. At both ends of the hall stood a fireplace. They were so poorly built that most of the smoke found its way into the room. A thick layer of soot covered the ceiling and walls. Weapons hung on the walls. The main table seated Cedric, his family, and important visitors. Other, smaller tables seated less-important guests.

The room was noisy and crowded. With a pang, Ivanhoe spotted Wamba, his father's court jester. Long ago, Cedric had chosen Wamba to watch over Ivanhoe. The two had spent many hours playing fetch and other games. Ivanhoe had laughed at all of Wamba's jokes. So had Cedric.

Tonight, Cedric was not smiling. He looked older. His yellow hair was streaked with gray. Still, he sat proudly, like a king.

He is every inch a leader, Ivanhoe thought. A lump formed in his throat. *And he is my father.*

Wamba wore colorful clothes of purple, red, and yellow. The floppy cap that sat upon his head was covered with bells.

"What do we have here, Uncle Cedric!" Wamba cried. He darted around Ivanhoe and the other strangers. He shook his cap of bells. "Behold, travelers who have courteously bathed before dinner. But they forgot to dry themselves off!"

The crowd laughed. Wamba held his nose, as if he smelled something very bad. Ivanhoe wondered if it was his own wet fur.

Then Wamba said, "They're Norman warlords whose fancy clothes still stink!"

Ivanhoe smiled. Jesters could tell the truth and get away with it. They worded all their remarks in a funny, almost clownlike way. That was why they were called jesters! Other people who dared to tell the same truths might very well end up in serious trouble.

"Humph!" Cedric, seated at the table in the place of honor, stared angrily at the newcomers. Ivanhoe longed to approach him and lie humbly at his feet. "The Saxon custom of hospitality requires that I welcome you."

Cedric clapped his hands. Servants approached and bowed, waiting for his orders.

In a noble voice, Cedric declared, "The night is bitterly cold. Goblets of fine hot spiced wine will warm your bones."

"That is nothing more than what you owe us," said the Norman knight. "I am Sir Brian de Bois-Guilbert. I have just returned from the war in Jerusalem. As such, you should treat me with all the courtesy I deserve."

"Humph!" Cedric said again. He pointed at Ivanhoe. "What of that man—the one who is so plainly clothed?"

Ivanhoe quickly lowered his muzzle. At all costs, his father must not recognize him. The thought filled Ivanhoe with sorrow.

"The Saxon is nothing to us," Sir Brian told Cedric. "We met him in the forest."

"A place must be made for him, as well," Cedric said gruffly.

Servants ran and fetched and brought food and drink. Ivanhoe's mouth watered. His nose filled with the rich smells of roasted pork, stewed rabbit, and sweets made with fruit and honey.

Ivanhoe sat on a big wooden chair at a small table. He lowered his head to lap up a drinking horn full of spiced wine. Then he noticed an old man who was standing a distance away from where he sat. The gray-bearded fellow was shivering with cold and had no place to sit.

Sighing, Ivanhoe jumped off his chair. He padded over to the man.

Ivanhoe said, "Please, sit at my place near the fire. I'm dry and warm now, and I have already eaten." Of course, none of that was true.

"Thank you, sir. Thank you." The man bowed again and again. He dipped so low that his long, smoke-colored beard nearly brushed the floor. His tall yellow hat finally fell off his head. He caught it and held it to his chest. "My name is Isaac of York. As you can see by my hat, I am a Jew."

Ivanhoe knew that people of the Jewish faith had a different religion and culture from most English people. For that difference, they were not trusted and were often hated. They were set apart as outcasts. To show that they were Jews, Jewish men were forced by law to wear tall yellow hats. Ivanhoe thought that the law and the treatment of the Jews were unfair.

Isaac continued. "I was traveling home to my daughter. She's alone, and I was worried. Then the storm threatened. I knew that Cedric would offer me food and shelter. But no one made room for me at any of the tables. Only you. I shall never forget your kindness, sir."

"Think nothing of it," Ivanhoe said. "I ask for nothing. You are a hungry man who needs protection. Before you, you see a poor stranger. But I am also a knight. It is my duty to see to your needs."

Isaac looked around. Many other knights were feasting in the great hall. "No one else appears to follow your code of conduct."

Ivanhoe lowered his head between his paws. "A great man taught me to live honorably and with courage." He was speaking of Cedric, but he dared not say his father's name aloud.

Suddenly, trumpets sounded as a side door opened.

"Behold the Lady Rowena!" Wamba cried, bending low.

Ivanhoe stopped himself from calling out to her with joy. Instead, he bowed over his forepaws with respect, as any stranger would.

Is she married? he wondered. *'Tis no matter. In any case, she is lost to me forever.*

She hadn't changed at all. She was still just as

beautiful as she had been years earlier. If anything, she was more enchanting than ever.

"Good evening to you all, my lords and ladies. And strangers," she said. For one moment, her eyes met Ivanhoe's. He knew she didn't recognize him. Yet he couldn't help himself from letting out a soft whine of greeting.

Then Ivanhoe's heart skipped a beat. In her right hand, she carried a red scarf. The letter "R" gleamed in silver and gold thread. It was the twin to the scarf that Rowena had given him. His was wound around his neck, under his clothes.

Isaac stared hard at Ivanhoe. He whispered, "I see that you wear a scarf exactly matching that of the fair lady. Is she your secret beloved, then?"

Ivanhoe realized that Isaac had spotted his scarf under the collar of his shirt. He turned his muzzle away so Isaac would not see the love for Rowena in his eyes.

The sounds of the trumpets died away. Rowena sat in a carved wooden chair beside Cedric. Food and drink were brought to her. But she left them untouched as she looked hard at Sir Brian de Bois-Guilbert.

"You've recently returned from the war?" she asked Sir Brian. Ivanhoe wagged his tail at the sound of her voice. "Can you tell me anything about a young knight named Ivanhoe?"

Cedric's face flashed with fury. His cheeks and forehead immediately burned a bright red. Ivanhoe's tail stopped wagging.

Sir Brian replied, "I know of him. He's a disobedient young Saxon knight. He was a coward, and a poor swordsman, too. I would like to meet him in combat someday. I would beat him easily."

Now Rowena looked angry. As Ivanhoe watched, she sat up straight and proud. She said, "In two days, there is to be a tournament at Ashby-de-la-Zouche. It's unfortunate that Ivanhoe still fights far away beside King Richard. He would certainly go to that tournament, and he would accept your challenge. And *he* would beat *you*."

Ivanhoe almost barked in agreement. He would win the day against this irritating man. It took all his youthful training for him not to flip in the air and cry out *"Woo-cha!* I accept your challenge!"

Instead, Ivanhoe stood alert. He leaned forward on his forepaws, as Cedric's grimace deepened. "Rowena," Cedric said harshly, "hold your tongue!"

"Hey!" Ivanhoe said, looking at Cedric. He took one step forward. Then he remembered that his identity must remain hidden. He fixed his gaze on Sir Brian as the knight laughed.

"I'm so much better than Ivanhoe that I would probably kill him," Sir Brian bragged.

Rowena's mouth opened with shock. Ivanhoe growled low and dangerously. No one heard him. Rowena said, "How can you speak of him so badly right in his father's house?"

Before Ivanhoe could stop himself, he barked, "He speaks like that because Ivanhoe is a fearless Saxon warrior! Sir Brian wants all the brave Saxons to die in the war. If that happens, then the Normans will rule in England without fear."

The angry knight drew out his sword. His men followed his lead. "You had better take care with what you say, stranger!" Sir Brian boomed. "I do not accept insults from my inferiors!"

Ivanhoe started to pull his sword from its scabbard. But then he stopped himself. His voice rang out once again. "If the true knight Ivanhoe were here, he would agree with me. And he would do something about all the injustices in this land."

"Yes!" Isaac of York agreed. He jumped to his feet. "Ivanhoe would most certainly defend all the weak and powerless!"

Ivanhoe raised his tail with joy. He had at least one supporter in the hall.

"You'll die for saying that!" Sir Brian shouted at Isaac.

Around the room, firelight flashed on a dozen sword blades. The knights prepared for a fight.

Cedric pounded the table with his hands. His fists echoed the wild beating of Ivanhoe's heart. "Enough! I will have no quarrels under my roof. Let no one speak of Ivanhoe in my presence. To me, he is dead." He stood up. His face was red with anger. "This feast is over."

Ivanhoe hung his head between his paws. He was as alone and friendless as a starving stray. Rowena also looked sad and troubled. With her head bowed, she followed Cedric. The two left the hall. Servants scurried to clear away the remains of the meal.

Then Ivanhoe's sharp sense of hearing picked up whispers. It was Sir Brian, speaking in a threatening tone of voice. Stealthily, Ivanhoe crept on all fours, his empty stomach brushing against the cold floor. His ears perked up as he came near the knight.

"We have been insulted," Sir Brian said angrily. "Isaac of York has had his last meal. I will kill him before this night is over!"

Ivanhoe cocked his head, listening hard. He was grateful for his good hearing.

One of Sir Brian's companions spoke up. "What of the Saxon stranger? He insulted us, too."

"We cannot anger Cedric," Sir Brian said. "He would not take kindly to the death of a Saxon. We'll make Isaac's death look like an accident. Then I'll hunt that Saxon down. I'll kill him after we're away from Rotherwood."

Just then, another of Cedric's old servants approached Ivanhoe. Ivanhoe almost gave out a happy yip. The man's name was Gurth. He was Cedric's pig herder. He was in charge of feeding all the pigs Cedric kept in pens outside the castle. Like Wamba, he had been Ivanhoe's friend since birth. He wore a strange garment made of animal hide. His hair was flaming red.

Gurth bobbed his head at Ivanhoe. He said, "If you please, stranger, come with me. I will herd you to a pen for the night." He flushed until his cheeks turned as pink as a newborn piglet. "I mean, I'll show you and Isaac of York to your rooms."

"That would be most kind of you," Ivanhoe replied.

Gurth found Isaac. The three walked through the mazelike hallways.

After some time, they were quite alone in a far corner of the big castle. Ivanhoe tugged with his teeth at Gurth's animal-hide garment.

"Look upon my face and you will know me," Ivanhoe commanded him.

Gurth bent down. He pushed the low-brimmed hat away from Ivanhoe's face. He studied Ivanhoe's features.

Gurth gasped. "It's my young master!"

"The great Ivanhoe!" Isaac said in surprise.

"Shh!" Ivanhoe warned them both. "Do you want to get us thrown in the dungeon—or worse? Don't even dare to say my name out loud. Now, listen, I've got to sneak Isaac out of here tonight. Gurth, you must help me in this task. Sir Brian has plans to murder him!"

"Oh, my poor daughter!" Isaac cried. He was holding his hat in his hands and was so nervous he twisted it. "I am all she has in this world. My horse's saddlebags hold gold coins and jewels. It is all yours if you will save me."

Gurth put his hands on his hips and cocked his head. "Didn't my master just say that he is going to rescue you?"

"Oh," Isaac said, startled. "Yes, he did." He clamped his mouth shut and stared at his ruined hat. Sighing, he tried to fluff it out and placed it on his head. It tilted at an angle just like the ruins of a castle turret.

"Peace, Gurth. This man is worried about his daughter." Ivanhoe felt a pain in his heart. He wished his own father cared as much for him as

Isaac did for Rebecca. "Isaac is a guest in the house of Cedric the Saxon. Cedric's son promises that no harm shall come to him."

"But you have no duty to your father," Isaac said. "He calls you his son no longer."

"Yet I am faithful to him," Ivanhoe replied. He touched his paw to his muzzle in a salute of respect. "Now, come, we must hurry."

Gurth shook his head. "It's too dangerous, master. We're locked in tighter than my porkers are in their pens. The whole land of England is filled with unrest and danger. Your father has placed guards at all the gates. By his strict orders, no one may leave the castle until morning."

"Well, we'll just have to find a way out, won't we, now?" Ivanhoe said bravely.

He waved his tail proudly like a flag. Then his fine sense of hearing picked up a noise.

"Hush!" Ivanhoe commanded. "I can hear someone coming!"

Ivanhoe grabbed Isaac's cloak between his teeth. He quickly led the elderly man behind a stone column and hid in the shadows.

A pair of heavy footsteps pounded on the hard floor. Gurth cleared his throat and said, "Who goes there?"

"Only a servant," came the reply. "I have been sent to find the stranger. The Saxon who traveled here with the Normans."

"Oh? For what reason?" Gurth's voice rose shrilly, betraying his feeling of terror. Ivanhoe could smell the man's fear.

"That is none of your business," said the voice. "I am ordered to fetch him at once, or there will be trouble. If you know where he is, tell me so."

CHAPTER FIVE

Ivanhoe followed the servant. The storm could be heard striking the thatched roof of Rotherwood. Wind whistled through the hallways of the ancient building. Ivanhoe shivered from the top of his head to the tip of his tail. His fur was still soaked through to his hide.

Zounds! I smell like a wet tapestry, he thought, as he looked at one of the wall hangings in the hallway.

The servant's torchlight threw the Saxon knight's shadow against the walls. The black silhouette showed a fierce, four-legged beast. Ivanhoe felt that danger lurked at every twist and turn. He had no idea when it would strike.

He growled deep in his throat. *I am prepared for danger,* Ivanhoe thought. *It's almost my middle name. But what about Isaac of York? The man is weak and helpless.*

Finally, the servant stopped in front of a heavy

wooden door. He knocked on it. It opened, and he went in. The door was then closed. Ivanhoe was left cooling his four paws. He wondered if the kitchen had saved any leftovers. He was so hungry that even a pre-bedtime snack would be welcome.

The door opened again. The servant poked his head out. "The one who wishes to speak with you waits inside."

How mysterious this is, Ivanhoe thought. *Well, it doesn't matter. I love a good mystery.* He trotted bravely into the room.

Rowena was sitting in a chair by a fire. She was so beautiful that he couldn't breathe for a moment. He could only wag his tail.

"Please, come closer," she said gently.

His heart spoke for him as he obeyed. *Whatever you wish. Just say the word: sit, stay, heel.*

"May I give you some wine?" she asked.

Got anything to go with it? he thought hopefully. *Rabbit? Roast pork? A meaty soup bone?*

"Thank you, my lady," he murmured. He kept his voice low. "You are most kind."

She didn't know who he was. With his paw, he touched his hat to make certain he was still properly disguised.

She has long forgotten me, he thought. *No doubt she has become Athelstane's wife.*

A pitcher and two glasses sat on a small table. The servant poured a goblet of wine. He put it down

in front of Ivanhoe. The Saxon knight began to lap at it. It was very spicy.

"Fetch meat and bread from the kitchen," Rowena told the servant.

Ooh, and dessert, Ivanhoe added silently. *Don't forget that!*

"As you wish, my lady." The servant bowed and left the room.

Ivanhoe was alone with Rowena. He struggled not to paw the earthen floor in his excitement, or, worse, do a flip.

"You spoke of Ivanhoe in the great hall. You must have been to Jerusalem," she began. She leaned forward. "What did you hear about the knight named Ivanhoe? Is he well? Is he alive?"

Her face spoke of her love for him. He wanted to shout "Rowena, here I am!" Instead, he took a deep breath. *She has to forget me.*

He said, "Sadly, I must tell you that he is dead."

Rowena burst into tears. "Oh, my Ivanhoe!" she cried. "No! I cannot believe it. Fate cannot be so cruel."

Ivanhoe shook his face free of wine droplets. He looked up at Rowena. "Your husband must be a comfort to you in this time," he said gently.

"Husband?" she cried. "I have no husband. I wait only for Ivanhoe."

Ivanhoe's heart skipped a beat. "You are not married?"

"Not yet, but that will come to an end soon." She buried her face in her hands. "I must marry Athelstane after the big jousting tournament at Ashby-de-la-Zouche!"

Ivanhoe swallowed hard. "Lord Athelstane is a noble man. He is the prince of all the Saxons."

"He is not Ivanhoe." Her voice was filled with sorrow.

Ivanhoe took a step forward on a shaky paw. He raised his right paw to comfort the young woman. She took it and held it tightly. He remembered the tender way she scratched between his ears.

"Often we sat, just like this," she said. "Ivanhoe and I, all alone, so happy."

Ivanhoe closed his sad eyes. *Yes, so we did,* he

thought. *In the dog days of summer. And winter. And spring. And autumn.*

The door opened. The servant had returned with Ivanhoe's meal. A huge platter was heaped with meats and delicacies he had not seen for years. But Ivanhoe no longer had an appetite.

He said, "Excuse me, my lady, but I must get some rest." He bowed over his forepaws. "Please," he said to the servant, "show me where I am to sleep. I understand I am to bed down near Isaac of York."

"They've put you near that outcast Jew?" the servant asked, surprised.

"Do as our guests asks," Rowena said. Her tears streamed down her cheeks.

Ivanhoe wished he could comfort her. If only he could tell her the truth. *But what good will it do? It will only make it harder for her to marry Athelstane.*

Upset and saddened, Ivanhoe circled left and walked out of the room.

He and the servant then made their way into another part of Rotherwood castle. His sharp sense of hearing picked up the echoes of Rowena's weeping. Her heart was breaking.

He whimpered gently. How could he let her marry another?

The servant led Ivanhoe to a room. It was dirty, wet, and cold. His sleeping area was covered with a pile of straw and a thin, ragged blanket.

"There are fleas all over here," Ivanhoe said. "This place isn't fit for man or beast!"

As soon as the servant was gone, he crept into Isaac's room.

Isaac's yellow hat of shame served as his pillow. The old man was bundled in his cloak, snoring loudly. Isaac might be a weak old man, but he snored like a lion.

Ivanhoe was glad that he had promised to protect Isaac. It gave him something to fill his mind. Otherwise, thoughts of Rowena would surely drive him mad.

She will be lost to me forever when the tournament is over.

Ivanhoe heard footsteps approaching. Quietly, he growled. Then he pulled his sword out from its scabbard. He quickly got down on all fours, ready to spring at whoever was coming.

"Sir Brian said to kill only Isaac," whispered a man in the darkness. "We are to take his money and jewels."

"What of the Saxon stranger?" a second man whispered.

"Sir Brian will kill him another time," the first man replied.

Ivanhoe growled. *Don't count on it, pal.*

"All right, then," the second man said. "Let's do it and have it over with."

Ivanhoe heard the scrape of metal. The men

were drawing their swords from their scabbards. The footsteps neared.

The two tiptoed into the room. It was dark, but Ivanhoe could hear their every movement. They began to creep through the straw on the floor.

"Woo-cha!" Ivanhoe shouted. He sprang at them, holding his sword firmly. He hacked and slashed without mercy, circling left, right, then left again. He flipped in the air.

"I'm wounded!" one of the attackers cried, as he fell to the floor.

"What's happening? . . . Where are you, Ivanhoe?" Isaac called out in the darkness.

Ivanhoe heard a sword strike the floor inches from his paws. *That's what everyone wants to know,* he thought.

There was another cry of pain. The second man also fell to the floor. He shouted, "Can this be the poor stranger? He fights like a warrior!"

"Not just like any warrior—like a purebred *Saxon* warrior!" Ivanhoe answered. "Isaac, I think our welcome has worn thin. Where are you?"

"Here, here," Isaac said.

"Grab onto my cloak. I'll lead you out of here," Ivanhoe told him.

The man reached out toward Ivanhoe's voice. He grabbed hold of Ivanhoe's clothing.

Ivanhoe raced out of the room. He ran as fast as

his four legs could carry him. Sir Brian's men moaned and rolled in the straw.

The first man cried out, "I'm wounded! And fleas are biting me!"

"Better start scratching!" Ivanhoe called over his shoulder. "Ha-ha! That'll teach them to mess with us, Isaac!"

"Oh, dear, oh, dear," Isaac murmured. He tried to put his yellow hat on securely as they ran. It kept falling off. He kept trying to put it back on. "Now they'll hunt us like foxes!"

"Ha! But we shall be fox *terriers*," Ivanhoe said, "and we will show our teeth!"

"Master!" someone cried.

It was Gurth, the faithful pig herder. He waved to Ivanhoe from an open doorway. He carried a small leather sack and a torch.

"Here is food for your journey," Gurth said. "Outside, two horses wait. You must avoid the night guards. Then your escape is certain."

"I thank you, my dear friend," Ivanhoe said. "Farewell."

Ivanhoe and Isaac hurried outside. The storm was fierce. The wind shrieked. A hard rain clattered on the mud like small, sharp stones.

Perhaps no one could hear our sword fight over the noise of the storm, Ivanhoe thought.

The horses were two of his father's finest. Ivanhoe helped Isaac mount his steed. Then he leaped atop his own. With a good strong bark, he shouted, "Follow me, if you wish to live!"

He and Isaac galloped into the storm-blasted night.

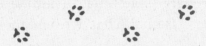

Ivanhoe and Isaac galloped until the horses panted with fatigue. Through forests and marshes, they rode at a brutal pace. Not once did they stop to look back to see if they were followed.

Then, at last, Isaac pointed to a distant light. "That is my home," he said. "My daughter will be waiting with worry for me."

Through the rain, Ivanhoe saw a large white building. The windows were golden with light.

Their horses clattered over the muddy ground and through the front gates. A man sloshed through the rain-soaked courtyard.

"My master!" he cried with joy. "When you did not come, we feared you were dead."

"This brave Saxon saved me," Isaac replied. He pointed to Ivanhoe as he got off his horse.

"Blessings on you, kind sir," the stable hand said gratefully.

The doors to the house opened. A lovely young woman with long black hair rushed out.

"Father!" Rebecca cried. She flung herself into Isaac's open arms. "I've been sick with worry."

"Sir Brian de Bois-Guilbert tried to murder me," Isaac said. "This man nearly died protecting me."

"It was nothing," Ivanhoe replied. He jumped off his horse. His four paws squished in the gooey mud.

"He is so modest." Isaac put his arms around the young woman. "So noble. Not like all those other Normans and Saxons."

"I am, however, just as muddy," Ivanhoe replied.

Isaac smiled at his daughter. "This is Rebecca."

"Welcome to our home, stranger," she said. She made a curtsy. "May you find peace here."

And something to eat, too, Ivanhoe added silently. *I am soooo hungry.* As Ivanhoe bowed over his forepaws, he said, "Thank you, Rebecca of York."

They walked into the house. In the main room, colorful pillows were piled high on beautifully patterned silk and wool carpets. Ivanhoe circled three times and then lay down among them. To his right side, a small brass table was filled with sweet-smelling plants. Curious, he sniffed at them.

"My daughter is a healer," Isaac of York said. "She grows herbs to use for natural healing remedies. If you are ever sick or hurt, she can cure you."

How useful, Ivanhoe thought. *But I hope never to have need of her services.*

Rebecca said, "We must repay you for saving my father's life. What can a simple Saxon wish for?"

"Full battle armor," Ivanhoe replied.

Rebecca's large, dark eyes widened. "But you are not a knight."

"This is Ivanhoe, the warrior champion of the Saxons," Isaac said. "He wishes to compete in the jousting tournament at Ashby-de-la-Zouche. He is dressed in this plain clothing so he will not be recognized." Isaac saw the puzzled look on Rebecca's face. "I'll explain later, my dear daughter."

"I have heard of you, sir knight," Rebecca said respectfully. "I bid you welcome. Of course we shall find you what you need." She smiled at him, her eyes shining. "And you shall have victory."

"Perhaps," Ivanhoe replied.

He thought of how Sir Brian had bragged that he would kill him. Then he thought of Rowena. And of his father, Cedric.

"I shall go in disguise," Ivanhoe told her. "No one must know my name."

Isaac made a face. "With Prince John as ruler, the contests have become very dangerous."

"Friend Isaac, fear not," Ivanhoe said, touched. "I have had a lot of practice with a lance."

Rebecca pressed her hands together. "I shall pray for you, Ivanhoe."

Isaac patted her hands. "My daughter is a woman of great faith."

Ivanhoe envied the love between Isaac and Rebecca. It reminded him of the love that Cedric had once had for him. *Isaac will love Rebecca always,* he thought. *He will never withdraw his feelings for her, no matter what.*

"In jousting tournaments these days, knights often battle to the death," Rebecca told Ivanhoe. "The Normans enjoy the drama and danger."

Ivanhoe lifted his muzzle. "It is a matter of honor," he said. "If death comes for me at Ashby-de-la-Zouche, so be it."

Rebecca looked unhappy. "But many will be saddened if that happens, I'm sure."

"No. No one will know who I am," Ivanhoe said sadly. "I am an outcast, just like you. My father has turned his back on me."

"I can't imagine such a thing," Rebecca said.

"I saw it with my own eyes," Isaac told her. "Such is the code of honor among the Saxons."

"I am a knight, and I am the son of a knight," Ivanhoe replied. "The weak and powerless need a champion. Saxon, Jew, and peasant—all of the underdogs in the world need to hope for justice. The Normans will not bully us forever."

"I shall pray all night for your safety," Rebecca said. "No sleep will close my eyes." She got up and left the room.

Alone now, Ivanhoe and Isaac faced each other. Ivanhoe's stomach growled.

"Uh . . . excuse me, but might I have a snack?" he asked Isaac.

Impressed, Isaac raised his eyebrows. "Only a very brave man could think of food at a time like this."

And a really, really hungry one, Ivanhoe added to himself.

Wow! It's hard to imagine what's going to happen when Ivanhoe competes at Ashby-de-la-Zouche. Before that battle begins, though, let's ride over to the next chapter and check on the competition already in progress at Sequoyah Middle School.

CHAPTER SIX

School was over for the day. The first round of the spelling bee was history.

Amanda walked away from Sam with a little smile on her face. Sam looked uneasy.

Sam's nervous, Joe thought. *She's afraid Amanda might be the best speller in our class. She doesn't want to let the team down.*

Joe and David went up to Sam. Joe said firmly, "Don't let Amanda get to you."

"Yeah," David chimed in. "You're just as good as she is. . . . Better," he added.

Sam smiled gratefully at her best friends. "Thanks, guys."

"We can go over to my house to study," Joe suggested.

Sam was an excellent speller, but even great spellers needed practice. David had also survived the first round. But he needed some help, too.

David looked eager to get to work. "Sure," he said.

Sam liked the idea, too. "Okay."

The three teammates left school to prepare for what they hoped would be victory.

Wishbone was sprawled on Joe's bed. It was time for his loyal subject—er, Joe—to come home from school.

Behold! he thought. *Lord Wishbone watcheth over ye Talbot domain! Let no man enter without permission!*

"And let no cat enter—no matter what," Wishbone added out loud.

His favorite toy, his squeaky book, rested securely between his front paws. *I'm really sinking my teeth into this book,* he thought. He chewed on the plastic toy with gusto. *And I feel almost as if I'm living Ivanhoe's story.*

Suddenly, Wishbone's sharp sense of hearing picked up the sound of footsteps. The front door opened. *Hark! Joe has cometh home!* He'd recognize his pal's movements anytime.

More steps followed. *Oh, boy! We have company!*

With a might spring, Wishbone jumped off the bed. The Jack Russell terrier trotted out of the room and down the hall.

"Comin' down!" he announced at the top of the staircase.

He began to race down the steps. With each bounding step the terrier took, his voice jiggled. "Hey-ey-ey-ey-ey-ey-ey-ey!"

Wishbone imagined himself on horseback, riding down a steep road. His lance was at his side. He was going to win the day.

He hopped off the last step and landed on the hardwood floor. He laughed and said, "I love that!"

Wishbone dashed into the study. Sam, David, and Joe had already settled down on the couch and a chair. Wishbone trotted past them and jumped up onto a footstool. He imagined victory. Then he claimed his big red chair.

"Okay, guys," he urged. "What's up?"

The three kids sat in silence. Joe was staring at a thin blue booklet. His two friends were staring at him.

"Okay, you two need to be ready tomorrow for

the second round of the spelling-bee contest," Joe said. "David, you get the first word."

David sat up a little straighter. He looked about as happy as Wishbone when he was at the vet's . . . getting a rabies shot!

Hmm . . . not at their happiest today, Wishbone thought. *They must be really worried about tomorrow's joust . . . er, I mean the spelling bee.*

"Per . . . *perspicacious,*" Joe announced.

Sam and David traded stunned glances. Sam frowned and gave her head a little shake.

"Ouch! That's a word?" Wishbone exclaimed. *I'm glad I'm a dog,* he thought.

"Joe, we're tired," Sam said. "Besides, we're not going to have words like *that* in the spelling bee."

Well, thank goodness, Wishbone thought. *The best place for a word like that is in the dictionary! I could eat a whole box of ginger snaps faster than it would take someone to spell a mouthful of a word like that.*

Joe shut the spelling booklet. He grinned and said, "It was funny to see Amanda's reaction when she started losing teammates."

The other two brightened up and chuckled.

"Did you see the look on her face?" David chimed in. He rolled his eyes and made a look of irritation. His expression resembled Amanda's so much that they all laughed.

Wishbone laughed, too. He had seen Amanda make that same face before.

"Ha!" he said, wagging his tail. He put his front paws on the arm rest and stood up. "It's probably a lot like the look that Sir Brian had on his face when Ivanhoe challenged the Normans in the joust."

Talk about a bad day for Sir Brian!

Wishbone let his imagination return him to the story of Ivanhoe.

Back to jousting! Back to knightly honor and glory!

CHAPTER SEVEN

At dawn the next day, Ivanhoe and his two new friends, Isaac and Rebecca, journeyed to Ashby-de-la-Zouche. The knight held the reins of a fresh horse between his teeth. His friends followed behind him.

Ivanhoe had put Cedric's two borrowed horses in the meadow near Gurth's pigsty. The two horses were too tired to continue to Ashby-de-la-Zouche. Ivanhoe trusted his old friend Gurth to round them up and return them to Cedric's stables.

The ride to the tournament was long and difficult. Now and then, Isaac asked to stop and stretch his legs. Ivanhoe agreed. He had four legs of his own to stretch. He wanted to be in tiptop condition for the tournament.

Sifting through all the forest smells, he pawed his way into some piles of leaves. There he found a few treats. *Bones! Yeah, snacktime!*

The three finally came to the top of the last grassy hill. Ivanhoe looked at the spectacle below.

The jousting field was a breathtaking sight. A rainbow of pennants and banners snapped in the breeze. The delicious scent of meat pies and roast pork filled Ivanhoe's nose. He also picked up the smells of horseflesh, sweat, blood, and dirt.

The peasants sitting high up in the wooden bleacher seats wore their coarsely woven clothing. The Norman nobles, seated up front, were dressed in their finest outfits. Seated among them, Prince John showed off his elegant royal clothing. Jeweled rings sparkled on his thick fingers.

Ivanhoe growled with anger upon seeing the ruler.

He taxes the poor people until they starve. Then he spends their money on his high-fashion clothes.

Ivanhoe's gaze shifted. Rowena and Cedric were seated with many other Saxons. Ivanhoe's heart filled with love.

To the right of Ivanhoe's father sat Athelstane. He was huge. Athelstane towered over his wife-to-be. His blond hair was wild and uncombed. His beard was littered with scraps of food.

The Saxon busily gnawed on a piece of meat. On his big lap, he balanced a huge platter heaped high with all sorts of treats. A tall drinking goblet sat at his side.

Athelstane would not compete in the joust today.

Or ever. He had not trained in knightly combat. For that reason, he was known as Athelstane the Unready.

He's sure not Athelstane the Underfed, Ivanhoe thought. The man stuffed half a loaf of bread into his mouth at once. He chewed with his mouth open. Then he picked up the goblet, leaned his head back, and drained every bit of liquid into his wide-open mouth. His happy burp vibrated over the murmurs of the crowd.

Ivanhoe ground his teeth. Tomorrow, this oaf would become Rowena's husband.

Ivanhoe said to Rebecca and Isaac, "I must take my leave of you. I cannot thank you enough for your many kindnesses."

Rebecca looked worried. She put her hand on his right paw and said, "Ivanhoe, I beg of you. Do not take part in this cruel sport. I fear you will die."

"Listen to my daughter," Isaac pleaded, nodding. His tall yellow hat bobbed like a chicken's head as he spoke. "She's as smart as she is beautiful. Such a wonderful young woman."

Ivanhoe was deeply touched by Rebecca's concern. He placed his left paw on her hand. "I have jousted all my life," he reminded her. "It's in my blood."

"Keep that blood inside your body," Isaac said nervously.

"I fully intend to," Ivanhoe said. Then he left his two faithful friends.

A short time later, Ivanhoe sat atop his fierce jousting horse. He wore full battle armor. The horse and armor were gifts from Isaac. Ivanhoe left his sword back at Isaac's home. Using that weapon in the tournament would have revealed his true identity. His family crest was on the handle of the sword. A picture of an oak tree with bare roots was painted on the shield he carried. His face was hidden by his helmet. No one would know that he was Ivanhoe.

Over the loud noise of the crowd, Ivanhoe was still able to hear bits and pieces of conversations in the stands. His father was complaining. "I watch this tournament and see only Normans. Normans, Normans, Normans! Everywhere, Normans. Is there no great and brave knight left to defend the honor of the Saxons?"

Cedric's court jester, Wamba, danced over to Cedric's seat. "Ivanhoe would be that worthy knight—if he were here."

Ivanhoe's ears perked up. He wagged his tail.

"Silence! Don't insult me!" Cedric bellowed. "Do not say that name in my presence—*ever*. Know this, Wamba. If you did not bring me such pleasure, I would have you silenced permanently."

Ivanhoe's tail drooped. *I have displeased my father greatly,* he thought. *He hates my loyalty to King Richard.*

He believes Rowena must marry Athelstane, although she loves me. We will never, ever understand each other.

Rowena's eyes filled with tears. Athelstane kept eating.

Then Isaac and Rebecca came near the crowd of Saxons. "Are there any seats for two tired travelers?" Isaac asked shyly. He took off his yellow hat and bowed.

Athelstane burped. "None," he said. He picked up an enormous greasy meat pie. As he ate, he smacked his lips and filled his beard with still more crumbs.

"Please." Rowena looked at Athelstane. "Let us show some kindness to these people. They look very tired."

They're dog-tired, Ivanhoe agreed. *They rode all day to get me to the joust on time.*

Isaac said, "We have a few coins. If I may pay for a place for my daughter?"

"Father, that is not necessary," Rebecca insisted. "No one else has paid." She said to Athelstane, "With due respect, my lord, there is room for us. All you need to do is move your goblet."

You go, girl, Ivanhoe thought. He admired Rebecca's spirit.

"How rude." Athelstane wiped his mouth with the back of his hand.

"Please, Athelstane. They look exhausted," Rowena said gently.

"Oh, very well." He picked up his big goblet. "I'll need a servant to hold this for me."

Ivanhoe clenched the horse's reins. He gripped the saddle angrily with his forepaws.

Then Prince John said, "It seems there are no Saxon contestants for today's tournament. So it shall be Norman against Norman."

"Not a single Saxon?" Cedric moaned.

Ivanhoe flicked the reins. With a snort, his horse galloped into the jousting arena. Ivanhoe raised his right paw in the air. He cried, "I am Saxon-born. I challenge *all* the Normans! Any Norman knight who wishes to fight me, give a shout!"

The crowd cheered. Ivanhoe galloped to the row of Norman shields on display. He grabbed his lance. He positioned it and held it steady. The weapon knocked over each shield as Ivanhoe thundered past.

A delighted cheer rose from the crowd. *Everybody loves a contest,* Ivanhoe thought.

Leaning over to the side, he let go of the lance. A servant took it away.

Prince John raised his hand, and the crowd fell silent. "You are brave but foolish, sir knight. You cannot possibly fight all the Normans here today."

Ivanhoe raised his muzzle. His dark eyes shone with determination. "I can—and I shall."

The crowd cheered again.

"Then make it so," Prince John commanded, raising his goblet to his lips.

"For the glory of England! For King Richard! For love, and for honor!" Ivanhoe cried. He rose from the saddle and balanced on his hind legs.

Don't try this at home, folks. I'm a professional.

"For the last day of your life," someone called. "For this is it, nameless Saxon knight."

Ivanhoe sat down on his hind legs.

Big surprise—it was Sir Brian de Bois-Guilbert who had just spoken.

Sir Brian sat astride the biggest horse Ivanhoe had ever seen. *Yikes! One crunch from one of those hooves, and I'm dog meat,* he thought.

Ivanhoe glared at his enemy. Then he remembered that Sir Brian couldn't see his face because of the helmet he wore.

He said, "I am Sir Disinherited. And, for your information, I won't be doing any dying today."

"Think you so?" Sir Brian said, sneering.

One by one, Norman knights rode up behind Sir Brian. Ivanhoe started counting them.

One . . . two . . . three . . . four . . . five . . .

"I didn't realize you Normans ran in packs," Ivanhoe said.

"Like wolves." Sir Brian chuckled. "You must defeat all of us to claim the victory. You yourself said it. Is that not so, Prince John?"

"That is so." Prince John shot an evil smile at Ivanhoe. "All of them. At the same time."

Ivanhoe was shocked by that. Ganging up on

an enemy wasn't fair. And knights were taught to fight fairly.

Prince John raised an eyebrow. "You are silent. Do you possibly wish to take back your challenge, Sir Sheep?"

Ivanhoe growled. "I am a Saxon knight. Never would I so dishonor myself."

"Well said!" Cedric cried. All the Saxons cheered and smiled. All except Rowena, who clasped her hands together.

Ivanhoe couldn't help himself. He gathered the reins. His horse crossed the arena to Rowena.

"My lady," he said, "I may die today. May I have something of yours to carry—for luck?"

She blushed. Then she took her red scarf from her cloak. "Wear this in memory of another brave Saxon knight. The knight known as Ivanhoe."

Clenching his jaw, Cedric looked away.

Ivanhoe leaned toward her. She wrapped the scarf around his neck. Her hands hesitated. He felt their coolness against his fur.

"I thank you, my lady," he said.

"Do you plan to dally all day?" Sir Brian boomed.

"Indeed not," Ivanhoe said. "I am not the dallying sort." He galloped to the opposite side of the jousting field. "Norman, prepare to be defeated!"

Sir Brian bellowed, "Saxon, prepare to die!"

The crowd went wild.

Athelstane pouted, saying, "I need more food. Is anyone listening?"

No one was listening. All eyes were glued to the two knights.

Storytellers will speak of this day, Ivanhoe thought. *Whether I live or die, my tale will be told.*

CHAPTER EIGHT

At Ashby-de-la-Zouche, the royal trumpets sounded. The crowd cheered wildly. Ivanhoe galloped off to one side of the jousting arena. The Norman knights galloped to the other side.

They turned their horses around to face each other. Their heads were protected by their helmets.

The trumpets stopped. Everyone fell silent. From the stands, sunshine glinted off the Normans' jewels and gold. The eyes of the Saxons glittered just as brightly.

Servants ran forward and handed lances to the Norman warriors. Ivanhoe had no squire, or servant, to help him. He sat atop his horse all alone, and unarmed. He had dropped his lance earlier.

"Unfair!" Rebecca of York cried and jumped to her feet. Her dark eyes flashed with anger. "This knight has no lance to defend himself. He is one against six. This fight is unfair."

The prince shrugged. "This nameless knight challenged Sir Brian. It is up to him to withdraw."

"He must have comrades to fight beside him," Rebecca insisted. "He cannot fight by himself."

Then Cedric rose like a mighty mountain. He cried, "The Saxons will rally around the disinherited knight!"

Cedric looked down at Athelstane. The large Saxon was eating another meat pie. He wiped his mouth with his wrist and burped.

Cedric fumed. "There are other Saxon warriors here." He looked around. "Are there not?"

No one spoke. No one moved. The Normans began to jeer and laugh.

"The Saxons are cowards," a man in velvet called. "No wonder we Normans rule England."

Prince John smiled.

This is not looking good, Ivanhoe thought. *I must do something.*

"One Saxon is enough to fight your war," Ivanhoe announced. His voice rang out loudly over the tournament field. "If it is necessary, I shall ride alone. For Saxon honor, I would singlehandedly challenge every Norman in England!"

The Saxons, nobles and peasants alike, burst into a wild round of cheering. Like a greased pig, Gurth the pig herder ran past the soldiers. He reached Ivanhoe's side. As Ivanhoe looked from his seat atop his horse, Gurth held out his hand.

"I shall fight with you," Gurth declared.

Ivanhoe waved his paw to a page and said, "Bring forth the horse I rode to this place."

Ivanhoe sighed. *In the right corner,* he thought, *weighing in at fourteen pounds, we have Kid Ivanhoe! And with him, wearing leather trunks, is an untrained pig herder on a tired old nag.*

Ivanhoe scratched his hindquarters. His chain mail was pinching his fur. Without thinking, Gurth reached up and scratched him. It reminded Ivanhoe of the old days at Rotherwood.

"Thank you, my friend," Ivanhoe said softly.

Gurth's horse was led into the arena. It dragged its hooves, clearly very tired.

Gurth mounted the exhausted beast.

"They must have help to arm themselves," Cedric said angrily. "Surely that is not against your rules, Prince John."

Ivanhoe's heart caught. *He does not know that he defends his very own son,* Ivanhoe thought. *Perhaps he would not ask for help for me, if he knew my true identity. Perhaps he would rather see me defeated.*

The thought was bitter.

"Very well," Prince John snapped. "Bring forth weapons for the Saxons."

A royal servant held out a lance to Gurth. It was like a long, thick pole. The tip was deadly sharp. Gurth's eyes bulged as he gripped the heavy weapon.

"Zounds! These things weigh a ton," he blurted out.

The tip of the lance stabbed into the ground. Sir Brian and the Norman knights laughed.

Rowena stretched out her lovely, slender hand. She said, "Blessings on you, Gurth. You are brave, indeed. Take care of this knight with the same skill you show in tending to our pigs."

Or with the same skill that Athelstane gives to his never-ending appetite. Ivanhoe thought. The prince of the Saxons looked like a chipmunk. Both of his cheeks were stuffed with food.

"Is there no one else who will join us?" Gurth said to the crowd.

The Saxon peasants moved forward eagerly. They pushed on the wooden wall surrounding the jousting field.

Prince John bellowed, "Enough! One insult to Norman knighthood is enough." He glared at Gurth. Then he looked over at the Saxon peasants. "There will be no more outbursts from low-born common folk."

"Then let the battle begin," Ivanhoe called. He raised his lance.

"As you wish." Prince John held his arm high, waving a colorful scarf in the air. It signaled that the contest would soon start.

The Normans prepared for battle. They aimed their lances at the hearts of their enemies. Ivanhoe did the same. The red cross on Sir Brian's armor was his target.

Suddenly, a hunting horn sounded. Everyone looked toward the sound. On the hill above the combat arena, men dressed in green stood in a row. One of them carried a large bow. A pack filled with arrows was strapped to his back.

"I am Robin Hood!" the man cried. "I live in the forest with my Merry Men. We are Saxons all. We will help the nameless knight."

Wow! Neat, Ivanhoe thought. He had heard of Robin Hood and his Merry Men. His tail wagged with joy.

"You are nothing but common thieves!" Prince John shouted.

"That is true." Robin Hood glared at the prince. "But we steal back what you take from the poor by force. You tax us Saxons to pay for all your flashy jewels. Meanwhile, our children starve."

"This is an outrage!" Prince John bellowed. "Guards, seize the outlaws!"

"No! Let them fight!" Rebecca cried.

"Let them fight!" Cedric agreed.

The crowd took up the chant.

Prince John frowned. "Oh, very well," he said.

Robin and his band placed arrows in their bows. *They have no horses,* Ivanhoe realized. *I will give Robin Hood my horse. I can fight on foot. After all, I have four to his two.*

But just then, Prince John dropped the scarf. The tournament had begun!

Shouting battle cries, the Norman knights dug their spurs into the horses' sides.

Ivanhoe couldn't help making a fierce bark in return. The fur rose along his back. He held his tail high with knightly pride.

His horse thundered toward the Normans. Gurth trailed behind. Ivanhoe's sharp sense of smell picked up the scent of fear. *Gurth is no warrior. Yet he risks his life for Saxon honor. What courage. What dedication.*

A rain of arrows shot into the shields of the Norman knights. *Robin Hood is using his bow,* Ivanhoe thought. *Good shooting!*

But no one was hurt. The Norman knights kept coming. Robin and his men were no match for knights on horseback.

Ivanhoe growled. *King Richard will punish his brother for allowing this unfair fight—if he ever returns from the war.*

Just then, a dark blur caught up with Ivanhoe's horse. It was a big black stallion. The horse carried a knight dressed all in black. Even the feathered plume on his helmet was black.

The mysterious figure pulled a sword and saluted Ivanhoe with it. Ivanhoe returned the salute with his lance.

Ivanhoe looked away from the black knight. Sir

Brian was almost within striking range of Ivanhoe's lance.

With tremendous strength, Ivanhoe smashed his lance into Sir Brian's shield.

"No!" Sir Brian roared. Dropping his lance, he fell backward off his horse.

As the crowd jeered, Sir Brian jumped to his feet. He drew his sword.

"I am not finished, Saxon!" he yelled at Ivanhoe.

No problem, Ivanhoe thought. He threw down his lance. Springing from his saddle, he made a four-paw landing on the dirt field. *Whoops. I'm not packing my sword,* he thought. *I dressed for jousting, not swordplay.*

At that moment, the black knight threw a fierce

weapon called a mace to Ivanhoe. The weapon had a short wooden handle with a chain that connected it to a sharp-spiked iron ball. Ivanhoe caught the mace's handle.

Sir Brian lunged. Ivanhoe blocked his thrust with a swing of the mace. Around them, the other Norman knights fought Ivanhoe's team.

Then Sir Brian staggered once, twice, and fell to his knees.

"Run him through!" Cedric shouted at the top of his lungs. The Saxons took up the cry.

"Nay, do not slay him, Sir Knight," Prince John said. His teeth were clenched and his face was red. "We declare him defeated."

The Saxons cheered.

Rebecca clasped her hands with relief and closed her eyes. She was praying.

Rowena smiled with joy.

Cedric raised his fists into the air.

Athelstane kept eating.

Ivanhoe looked for the black knight, but the helpful stranger was gone.

Gurth limped toward Ivanhoe, a happy smile on his face. "We did it!" he said. His smile was huge. "You, me, and Robin Hood." He looked around. "Where is Robin Hood?"

The brave Saxon and his band were gone.

"We will find them," Ivanhoe told Gurth. "We will thank them properly, like true knights."

Gurth stood tall and proud. "Me, a knight? I wish that were so."

"You have the heart of a knight," Ivanhoe told his friend.

With a long face, Prince John rose. He held out a laurel wreath, the symbol of victory. "Disinherited knight, we hereby award to you the full honors of this tournament." He sighed.

Ivanhoe bent his head to receive the wreath. Suddenly he felt very dizzy. He looked down and saw that he was covered with blood. His own.

There was a huge slash across his right side. Blood poured from it. He was also injured across his chest and his right forepaw. *I'm wounded.* In the heat of combat, he had not felt any pain. Now he did. The gash was very deep.

With a groan, he fell down.

The crowd pushed forward. Cedric and Rowena rushed to Ivanhoe's side. They crouched over him. With blurry eyes, Ivanhoe gazed up at them.

Loyal Gurth removed his friend's helmet.

"Ivanhoe!" Rowena cried with shock. "Cedric, it is your son!"

"Father . . ." Ivanhoe whispered. His voice was weak. "Before I die, call me your son again."

Cedric stared down at him. Tears filled his eyes. His lips trembled as if the words hung on them. Then his face hardened. His eyes went cold. "I have no son," Cedric said quietly. He rose to his feet and walked away.

"Cedric, he is dying!" Rowena pleaded. "Let him die with peace of mind." She placed her hand in Ivanhoe's paw. "Do not leave me, my love. I beg of you, live."

Rebecca knelt beside Rowena. She touched Ivanhoe's wounds. He gasped. "Father, I must help him, or surely he will die."

"I fear for you if you do such a thing," Isaac said. "Prince John will not think kindly of it if you use your healing powers to cure him."

"But he *must* live," Rebecca insisted.

"He *must* live," Rowena echoed, as she knelt beside Rebecca.

"Gosh, ladies, I'll do my best," Ivanhoe said, gasping. Then he fainted dead away.

Wow! Sir Walter Scott really knew how to end a chapter! No wonder so many people love to read his novels. I wonder how things are going back in Oakdale. Let's find out!

CHAPTER NINE

At the Talbot house, Wishbone was about to faint dead away—from hunger. He dozed in his big red chair. His three friends were still working on their spelling. But they sounded like they'd had enough practice.

"Hey, guys," Wishbone said. "I could use a little pick-me-up." He jumped off his chair and sat in the center of the room. "What do you say?"

"I'm hungry," Joe said.

Wishbone was pleased. "And I thought no one would ever listen to the dog!"

Sam said, "Me, too."

Good. That means we have a majority. I'm thinking ginger snaps.

"We've got to keep studying," David insisted.

Sam gave her head a little shake. "I can't. I'm exhausted." She looked frustrated. "Face it. We're doomed."

David thought a moment. Then he said, "Wait a minute." He opened up his backpack. He pulled out something that smelled delicious.

Wishbone perked up as his nose picked up the scent.

David handed a yellow packet to Sam. "Here," he said. Then he tossed another packet to Joe. "Did you ever try these snack bars?"

"Ooh," Wishbone said, standing and stepping forward.

"My mom always buys them," David continued. All three kids started opening the wrappers. "She says they're good for giving you energy."

"I'm all for energy," Wishbone said eagerly.

"Great," Sam said.

"Uh . . . excuse me, but this food intermission

was *my* idea," Wishbone reminded them. He pawed the air. "Where's the snack bar for the dog?"

The three kids started eating the bars.

"Helllooo! There is someone in this room without a snack. Argh! What does a guy have to do to get some attention around here?" He barked.

Joe nodded as he chewed. "Not bad."

"Yeah, it's pretty good," Sam agreed.

"I'm begging," Wishbone said.

"What's in them?" Sam asked.

"Let's see." David smoothed out the wrapper so that he could read the list of ingredients. "Wheat, rolled oats . . ."

"I'm still begging . . ." Wishbone patiently reminded them.

"Honey," David continued, "coconut . . ."

Sam gasped. Watching her, Wishbone dropped his front legs to the floor. He murmured, "Uh-oh."

"Fruit topping," David continued reading, "concentrate . . ."

Wishbone wagged his tail anxiously. He stepped forward, his eyes on Sam.

"*What?*" Sam cried.

David stopped reading. "What?" he echoed.

Joe looked at Sam. "Are you okay?"

Wishbone cocked his head to one side. "I'm not sure if she is. She does look a little green."

Worriedly, Sam asked, "Did you say *coconut?*"

"Yeah," David answered. "Why?"

"I'm allergic to coconut!" she told them.

Joe's voice rose with worry. "Like how? What happens?"

"My nose gets all stuffed up," she said unhappily. "My eyes start itching, and my skin breaks out. Sometimes I get all puffy."

"Do we need to call a doctor?" Joe asked.

"I don't know," Sam admitted. "Sometimes it takes a while for the symptoms to show up."

"Okay, well, let's not panic," David cautioned. "Maybe nothing will happen."

As if in reply, Sam sneezed.

"Uh-oh," Wishbone said. "Initiate allergy panic alert," he announced. He began circling right. "Woo-ooh-woo-ooh!" He howled like an ambulance siren. "Remove all coconut-bar treats from the building!"

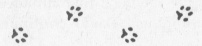

What's going to happen to Sam? What's happening to Ivanhoe? Whew! The tension's driving me crazy! Let's check on our brave knight!

CHAPTER TEN

Ivanhoe slowly awoke. His chest and sides were tightly wrapped up with bandages. Weak and fuzzy—*not to mention furry*—he lay in a horse-drawn wagon. He was hidden from view by a cover laid over the wagon.

As the wagon rolled along on its rickety wooden wheels, the bouncing and rocking caused him great pain. But he was a knight. Knights were used to pain.

His nose told him he was in a forest. He smelled dark, damp earth, fragrant ferns, and trees. Lots of trees.

Hmm . . . I could really use a tree right about now, he thought.

But he was so weak, he could barely even lift his head.

The wagon shot forward. Then it jerked to a sudden stop. A loud crack sounded. The wagon tilted dangerously to the right. Ivanhoe was tossed against the side.

The flap of the wagon cover opened. Rebecca appeared, dressed for travel in exotic silk robes. A silk cloak was draped around her shoulders, and a stylish turban crowned her head.

"Ivanhoe?" she asked. "Are you injured even more?"

"What happened?" he questioned.

Rebecca sighed. "One of the wagon wheels broke. My father is too weak to repair it alone."

"I shall help him do the repair," Ivanhoe said. He tried to get to his four feet, but his bandages were too tight. "Have you treated my wounds?" he asked her.

"Yes." She placed her hand on the side of his muzzle. "You must rest. Sir Brian's sword slashed you deep. You have lost much blood."

He put his paw on her hand. "You are an angel of mercy. Twice now, the Yorks have saved my life. I am forever in your debt."

Rebecca's smile was gentle. "You are truly a great hero, Ivanhoe. To both Saxon and Jew alike. You defend those whom no one else cares about. You stand for justice."

"Hey, it's just what I do," he said modestly.

The pounding thud of approaching horses' hooves silenced them both. Rebecca's eyes widened with concern.

"Are you expecting company?" Ivanhoe asked.

Rebecca shook her head. "Perhaps we are about to be set upon by robbers."

"It could be Robin Hood and his men." He reached out to grab his sword. But then he remembered that he had left his sword at Isaac's house.

"Are you looking for this, Ivanhoe?" Rebecca held a sword.

"It is not mine," Ivanhoe said.

Rebecca said, "It was left to you by the black knight, and I will use the sword, if I must."

He was impressed. Rebecca was one brave woman. "Take care, fair maid. It is probably very heavy," he warned her.

She wrapped one hand around the hilt. Her eyes widened. Then she used her other hand to get a firm grip on the weapon. Straining, she slowly began to lift the sword.

The sound of the hooves grew louder. Ivanhoe said, "Pray, do not try to use the sword. It is too heavy for you. You cannot hope to change the odds if there is a fight."

Rebecca lifted her chin. "My people are used to bad odds, Ivanhoe. Yet we survive and thrive."

With that, Rebecca closed the flap. She left the wagon.

Cast into dim shadow, Ivanhoe listened hard.

"Hello, there!" cried a very familiar, joking voice. Bells jangled. "What is this? Master Yellow Hat is a wagon mender."

That's Wamba, Ivanhoe thought. He wagged his tail. *Rowena and my father must be with him.*

"What has happened to your wagon?" another speaker asked. It was Cedric!

Ivanhoe wagged his tail even harder. "Father," he whispered.

"Good sir," Isaac said, "once before you gave me aid. My daughter and I are traveling home. But, as you see, our wagon wheel is broken. We are fearful of the forest. Would your bravery perhaps help us once more?"

"Humph!" Cedric said.

Ivanhoe pawed the wagon floor, struggling to rise. He failed.

"The man is old and weak," Wamba said. "The maiden is brave and beautiful. We cannot leave them in this dangerous situation."

"Somebody has been following us, Cedric," another voice chimed in.

Ivanhoe's tail picked up speed. It was the voice of his one true love. "We cannot leave them here with this broken wagon. They are helpless."

Ah, my sweet Rowena, Ivanhoe whined gently to himself. *She is always so kind . . . so thoughtful.*

"If we delay, we may be late for your wedding," Cedric replied. "Athelstane awaits us at his castle."

Rowena was still not married! *Do the delay thing, Father. Take all the time that you need,* Ivanhoe urged silently. *Hours. Even days.*

"I ask you not for myself," Isaac said, "but for my daughter. My every thought is for her."

Ah, Ivanhoe thought, *if only my father still cared that way for me.*

"Very well," Cedric said. "It is a good man who looks after his child so well. We shall fix your wagon. Then you may join us on the road."

"You are too kind," Isaac said.

"It is my duty to help those in need." Cedric's voice was gruff.

"Like me, Father. We are so much alike," Ivanhoe whispered. "We are united in purpose, but not in your forgiveness."

Suddenly, the air echoed with shouts and hoofbeats. Rowena screamed.

Then a man shouted, "Cedric the Saxon, put down your weapon!"

Ivanhoe could not stand his own weakness any longer. Gritting his teeth, he made one last effort to stand. The bandages stretched and strained his wounded body. His gash burst open. His fur was soon soaked with blood.

Still, the brave knight managed to drag himself to the back of the wagon. With his teeth, he opened the heavy flap.

Sir Brian de Bois-Guilbert was sitting proudly on his battle horse. The Norman knights from the tournament surrounded him.

Cedric was dragged forward by two men on

foot. His hands were tied. He said, "In the name of justice! Why are we to be prisoners?"

Sir Brian sneered at Cedric. "That concerns you not at all, you miserable Saxon! Away with you!"

Ivanhoe growled deep in his throat. His father was dragged out of sight.

"We shall take them to Castle Torquilstone," Sir Brian said.

Ivanhoe tried to raise a paw in protest. Castle Torquilstone was a dreaded ruin of a place. *It's worse than that fleabag room I stayed in at Rotherwood,* he thought.

Sir Brian added, "Cedric's friends will pay a large ransom for his safe return."

"And what of the Lady Rowena?" asked one of Sir Brian's men.

The fur on Ivanhoe's back stood up. He was furious enough to bite. *Rowena!*

"She must not marry Athelstane," Sir Brian replied. "The Saxons must have no hopes of ruling England again." He smiled cruelly at one of his men. "Perhaps *you* should marry her."

Ivanhoe growled again.

Just then, Rebecca and her father were led to Sir Brian. The sword Rebecca carried was taken away from her. As Ivanhoe looked on, the evil knight's eyes lit up. His lips parted.

"Who is this beauty?" he asked, drinking in the sight with his eyes.

"She is my daughter. Touch her and you will die!" Isaac shouted.

"Nonsense." Sir Brian leaned forward. He held out a hand. "Ride with me, fair one. The way to Torquilstone is long."

"Never." Rebecca lifted her chin in challenge.

Sir Brian frowned. "If I say that you will ride with me, you shall." He grabbed her hand roughly and pulled her up behind him. Then he pointed at the wagon. "What's in there?"

Rebecca took in a deep breath. "Nothing of any value."

Sir Brian narrowed his eyes. "Perhaps I should investigate. We'll see if you're telling the truth."

He got off his horse and began to walk toward the wagon.

CHAPTER ELEVEN

The next morning, Wishbone, Joe, and David walked toward Sam's house. This was the second day of the spelling-bee contest. It was down to two people on each team. Wishbone moved his four legs quickly to keep up. The boys were eager to know if Sam was all right.

Wishbone knew how they felt. The nearer they got to Sam's, the more worried the terrier became. If Sam was sick, Team A would lose its top speller. David would be the only member of the team left standing. Team A could end up in the doghouse.

"Today, on *Wishbone Live*," Wishbone announced, "our topic of discussion will be allergies. We'll talk about the people who have them, and the people who live with them."

The suspense was getting to the dog. It seemed to take forever until the group finally arrived at Sam's front door. Joe knocked.

Sam's dad opened the door. "Good morning," Mr. Kepler said. "Come on in."

"Hi, Mr. Kepler," Joe said. The two boys walked into the house. Wishbone trotted in after them.

Mr. Kepler was a nice man. He gave Wishbone the run of the house. And he usually had great snacks on hand.

None of them with coconut, Wishbone thought.

"We decided to stop by and walk Sam to school," Joe explained.

"It was actually my idea," Wishbone added.

David swallowed hard. "Please say that Sam's coming to school," he begged. "Please?"

At that moment, Mr. Kepler moved to shut the door. Sam stood right behind him. Her face was red, swollen, and blotchy.

"Sam?" David said, shocked.

Wishbone gasped. With his paw, he covered his eyes and turned away. "Say it isn't so!"

"I'm sorry, Sam. I'm really sorry," David said to his friend.

"It's not your fault. It was an accident." Her voice was hoarse. It was the way Wishbone's voice sounded after he had a good, long barking spree.

Not that I would be so rude, he thought. *I am not a barking-spree kind of dog . . . well, unless cats stuck in trees are involved.*

"Unfortunately, I don't think Sam will be going to school today, guys," Mr. Kepler said.

"Uh-oh," Wishbone murmured. "Now our worst fears have come true."

Sam walked over to the couch and she plopped herself down on it.

"Sorry, Sam." Mr. Kepler went and sat beside his daughter.

"Amanda's going to think I panicked and didn't want to show up on purpose." Sam sounded very upset as she spoke to the boys. She turned to her father. "She's going to think I'm scared."

"It really doesn't matter what Amanda thinks." Mr. Kepler's voice was soothing, but firm. He smoothed Sam's ponytail as he spoke comfortingly to her. "Your only assignment today is to get well."

David made a face. "It hurts just to listen to your voice—no offense."

I agree, Wishbone thought. *And I've got the most forgiving ears in this room.*

Sam leaned forward. She looked hard into David's eyes. "David, you've got to go all out for our team and win the spelling bee."

Wishbone could smell David's fear.

"Me?" David asked. He aimed a glance toward Joe. Then he sighed. "Yeah. Right."

"I *know* you can do it," Sam insisted. "If anyone can, it's you."

"Of course he can." Joe looked eagerly at David. "My dad used to tell his basketball players that you just have to swallow your fear and do your best for the good of the team."

Wishbone caught Joe's sense of excitement. He pawed David's jeans leg as a sign of support. "That's right! Believe in yourself, David! You can do it!"

"Well, okay . . ." David sounded a little more hopeful. He looked as if he was thinking hard. "Okay, I'm gonna do it," David finally said.

Wishbone was pleased. "You know, I'm pretty good as a motivational speaker."

David said, "Well, so long for now, Sam. Take care of yourself."

"I really hope you get better soon," Joe added.

Sam walked them to the door. "Thanks—and good luck!"

Wishbone dashed out with the boys. He herded them down the sidewalk.

"That's it, boys!" he urged them in a confident voice. "Chests out. Chins up. Onward and upward to victory!"

Then he slowed down and sat back on his haunches for a few moments. With a sigh, he watched the boys trudge toward school with their shoulders slumped.

"I hope they know what they're doing," the terrier muttered to himself. "They're in for the battle of their lives."

Wishbone stood up and trotted at a good pace. He caught up with the boys as his four legs moved briskly. He kept his tail high and self-assured. He knew he had to cheer his friends on.

"Okay, boys, remember, have confidence!" he reminded them. As they neared school, they bumped into Nathaniel Bobelesky and Amanda. They were the last two competing members of Team B.

"Oh, the Normans!" Wishbone cried. "Uh . . . I mean, the enemy."

Amanda looked at the boys. "Where's Sam?"

"Uh . . . Sam?" Joe echoed. "She couldn't make it today."

Amanda grinned smugly.

"Yeah. She's sick," David added.

"Oh, really?" Amanda didn't sound as if she believed the excuse.

"Really." Joe was firm.

"Well, this sort of changes the odds of the

spelling bee." Amanda already sounded certain of victory.

"David can do it," Joe said confidently.

Yeah. Wishbone wagged his tail. *He sure can!*

Mr. Pruitt appeared. "All right. Three minutes to the bell. Let's go." With a spring in his step, he opened the school's front door.

"Go, boys! Hey, team! Hey, team! Hey, team! Ha-ha!" Wishbone cheered. He sat at the end of the sidewalk. He said, "There's got to be a way I can get in on this action."

Wishbone thought for a moment. He came up with a battle plan.

Wagging his tail in a friendly way, he spoke more loudly. "Uh . . . Mr. Pruitt," he called out. "I know it's highly unusual, but I was wondering if I . . ."

Mr. Pruitt stepped inside the building and shut the door.

"I guess not . . ." Wishbone finished sadly.

He sat for a moment.

"Humph! I *can't* miss this competition."

The terrier trotted over to one of the outdoor lunch tables. He hopped up and lay down.

"Boy," he said, "now I know how Ivanhoe felt. He was cooped up in that terrible castle while all the action was happening somewhere else."

CHAPTER TWELVE

As Sir Brian approached, Ivanhoe crouched down in the wagon. He needed his sword. Well, not *his* sword, actually. It was the one that the black knight had lent him.

I should not have let Rebecca take the sword, he thought. *Had I a weapon, I could save everyone, even if I died in the attempt.*

"Hark! Sir Brian, Cedric's jester has escaped!" cried a Norman knight.

Go, Wamba, Ivanhoe thought. *Sound the alarm. Get help!*

"After him!" Sir Brian bellowed. "You fools!" Sir Brian yelled at his men.

He slammed his fist down on the wagon, then stomped away.

The jangle of spurs and armor clanged like church bells. Horses' hooves thundered as Sir Brian shouted, "Stop the jester! Kill him if you find him."

"I pray you, please do not harm him," Rowena begged.

As Ivanhoe lay inside the wagon listening, he realized that he was still bleeding. His white paws were splattered with the red drops.

"Why should I spare him, Lady Rowena?" Sir Brian asked coldly. "He means me no good. Why not rid the world of him?"

Rebecca was not afraid to speak up. "Because he is a brave man. And all brave men everywhere deserve to live."

Ivanhoe gave a low bark of agreement. *You tell him, Rebecca!*

Sir Brian said, "So you also plead for him, lovely one. Let me prove my love for you. I hereby decree that he shall live."

"Thank you, sir knight," Rowena said.

"I doubt your promise, Sir Brian," Rebecca insisted. "Tell the others to spare him. Now."

Ivanhoe raised a weak paw as a salute. *Rowena is so kind. Rebecca, so strong. And neither one is afraid to show it, either.*

His breathing was shallow. His vision began to blur. His wound was deep and painful.

I may be dying. If that be so, I bid my true love farewell. Perhaps in a better world, we shall be together, Rowena.

Ivanhoe felt his life slipping away from his body. Then everything faded to black. . . .

When Ivanhoe finally awoke, a blurry face looked down upon him. He blinked and said, "An angel?"

"No, it is I, Rebecca," she answered, as she sat next to him. "I was allowed to save you. You lay near death, Ivanhoe."

"You possess the power of healing. I am most grateful, dear Rebecca."

He laid his paw on her hand. She smiled gently.

She said, "My knowledge of healing is a gift from God."

"I remember little since Wamba fled. Was he caught?"

She smiled. "He was not."

He nodded. "We have hope of help, then."

Ivanhoe looked around. The room was round and built of large stones. Green moss covered some of the gray blocks. A tiny window slit let in dull, foggy light. There was one door, and it was closed.

"So, this is Torquilstone," Ivanhoe said. "Not exactly a cheery place."

"We have been prisoners in here for days," Rebecca told him. "Your father, and mine, too. And your lady love."

Ivanhoe said, "I must save us all."

He struggled to sit, but he could not raise himself up. Rebecca withdrew her hands. He glanced down at his body. He was shocked. His bandages were gone. Some of his fur had been shaved away. On his side, his wound had been sewn together like clothing. Another cut crisscrossed his chest. A third had slashed his right forepaw.

"Avoid movement," Rebecca said. "You must do nothing but rest."

"I cannot rest," Ivanhoe insisted. "We must be gone from here."

She put her hand on the top of his head and scratched. "I pray you, stay calm."

The bolts on the outside of the heavy wooden door were suddenly pulled back.

Rebecca's eyes grew huge. She paled. The hand she had placed between Ivanhoe's ears trembled.

"I shall protect you," Ivanhoe promised. *Or I'll die trying.*

"No. I beg of you, just pretend to sleep." She frowned at him. "I beg you, please."

"It is against my nature to hide from danger."

Rebecca placed her hand on his muzzle. "It is my heart's request," she said.

The door opened. Rebecca stood up and walked toward it.

"Rebecca."

The fur on Ivanhoe's back stood on end. He pretended to be asleep. He forced away the growl that was forming in his throat. It was his mortal enemy, Sir Brian de Bois-Guilbert. He entered the room, then slammed the door behind him.

"Rebecca, as is my custom, I have come to beg," Sir Brian said.

If I throw you a stick, will you leave? Ivanhoe thought.

"Love me, and then I will spare Ivanhoe and his family."

"Each day you promise me that. And each day I refuse," Rebecca said.

"Then I shall kill Ivanhoe now," Sir Brian said.

Ivanhoe heard the sound of a sword being pulled from its scabbard.

"He lies near death," Rebecca protested. "You

will dishonor your knighthood if you choose to kill a defenseless dying man."

"My hatred for him runs deep. He made me look like a fool."

Then Ivanhoe did let out a growl. Rebecca quickly covered the sound by coughing.

"Then the other Saxons in this castle will die."

"I do not believe it," Rebecca said, holding her head high. "You are a knight. You have honor. You have sent demands for payment in exchange for their safe return."

"No one has yet answered my demands," Sir Brian said. "That proves Cedric's followers care not if he dies."

"The king will punish you when he returns from the Crusade." She backed up toward Ivanhoe with her hands behind her back. She signaled with her hands for Ivanhoe to stay down.

With great effort, Ivanhoe raised his head and licked her fingertips. He wanted to show that he would defend her.

But I lie here like a sick child, he thought.

Sir Brian chuckled. His footsteps creaked on the floor. "King Richard is not here. Prince John will not punish me if I kill Saxons."

The Norman came ever closer toward Rebecca with his arms open. She raised a hand to strike him.

There was a shout. The door burst open. One of Sir Brian's knights panted in the doorway. Ivanhoe smelled fresh blood on the man's wounded arm. He had been shot with an arrow.

"Sir Brian!" the knight shouted. "We are under attack!"

"We are saved!" Rebecca cried with joy. "I have prayed for this!"

"Keep praying, fair Rebecca," Sir Brian replied. "Your rescuers are doomed. This castle is a mighty fortress. My Norman knights will defend it to the death."

"But the power of justice is on our side," Rebecca said firmly. "You will see."

"I will see your heroes *dead*," Sir Brian replied.

Sir Brian and the other knight left the room. The castle filled with the sounds of shouts and the ringing of swords.

Ivanhoe gritted his teeth, frustrated. "I am useless," he moaned. "Pray, tell me of the battle."

Rebecca ran to the narrow window. She looked out and surveyed the scene down below.

"Oh!" she cried. "The black knight heads an army!"

"The warrior who fought beside me at Ashby-de-la-Zouche?" Ivanhoe wagged his tail. "He is a stranger to me. And yet he risks his life again for me and those so dear to my heart."

"Arrows are flying!" she reported to Ivanhoe. "It is Robin Hood and his Merry Men. They are shooting flaming arrows at the castle."

"If I could only fight," Ivanhoe said angrily. "Rebecca, can you not make a potion that will give me strength?"

"I will not," she said, turning to look at him. "If you fight, you will surely die. You are gravely wounded already."

"Better to die fighting with knightly honor—"

Suddenly, a loud noise cut through the air. Ivanhoe smelled smoke.

Uh-oh. Not a good thing, he thought.

Rebecca turned back to the window. She gave a little cry of fear.

"The castle burns!" she cried.

Just then, their prison of a room burst into flame. The doorway was ringed with fire. The wooden door fell off its hinges and crashed into the room.

"Fly, Rebecca!" Ivanhoe urged her.

"I will not leave you!" Very frightened, she rushed to his mattress, sat down, and cradled his paw gently in her hands.

Angry flames of fire shot up through the wooden floor and began to lick at the walls. The damp moss on the stones sizzled, then burned. Ivanhoe felt the intense heat and began to pant.

"Rebecca, away with you!" Ivanhoe ordered.

"No, sir knight, I shall not go," she insisted.

Sir Brian staggered into the room. His armor was broken. His helmet was gone, and his hair hung

wild and tangled. Blood and soot were streaked across his face.

Not a good look for him, Ivanhoe thought.

"Rebecca, there is but one path to safety," Sir Brian said. He held out his hand.

She raced back toward the window. "I will never go with you! I would rather leap to my death!"

Sir Brian ignored her. He grabbed her wrist and dragged her away from the window and through the doorway.

"Traitor!" Ivanhoe shouted. With every last bit of his strength, he sprang to his four legs. His tail extended high behind him, a sign of his courage. "Set her free! Ivanhoe commands thee!"

The only answer he received were Rebecca's fading screams.

The villain has captured her. I have failed her, Ivanhoe thought.

"Farewell, Father. I love thee, Rowena," he whispered.

His tail drooped. He began to sway.

The fire raged all around him. Parts of the cot were burned as black as the tip of his nose. The heat was scorching.

I always believed that I would die old, Ivanhoe thought.

Then, after he had one final thought of Rowena, Ivanhoe collapsed.

Ivanhoe is trapped in a burning tower room in Sir Brian's castle. He desperately wants to rescue his lady love, Rowena; his father, Cedric; Rebecca; and Isaac. But he can barely move a muscle. Talk about being in the hot seat!

Speaking of having the heat turned up, I wonder how David's taking the pressure of the spelling bee back in Oakdale. Let's find out!

CHAPTER THIRTEEN

From his resting place on the lunch table, Wishbone rose up. "Hmm . . ." he said. "I wonder how it's going in there."

By "there," he didn't mean Castle Torquilstone. He meant Sequoyah Middle School. *David's probably sweating as much in there as Ivanhoe is in the burning castle tower.*

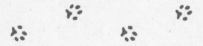

Joe could see the tension written all over David's face. It was Nathaniel and Amanda against him.

Go, David! Joe silently urged his friend.

"Camouflage," Mr. Pruitt announced clearly to Nathaniel.

Nathaniel didn't seem very happy. He looked as if he had no idea how to spell the word. He said, "Camouflage . . . C-a-m-a-f-l-o-g-e."

Amanda made a face.

"I'm sorry," Mr. Pruitt said kindly. "But that is incorrect. Take your seat, please."

Nathaniel sat down.

The teacher looked at David. "It looks like we're down to the final round. The teams are tied. There's only one member left for each side."

We know, we know, Joe thought anxiously.

"Are you ready?" Mr. Pruitt asked David.

David froze for a moment, then nodded.

"David, your word is *camouflage.*"

David cleared his throat. *"Camouflage,"* the boy repeated. "C-a-m-o-u-f-l-a-g-e."

"Yes, that is correct," Mr. Pruitt announced.

Joe and the rest of Team A applauded and cheered. Relieved, David grinned at Joe.

"That one was for Sam," David said.

"Amanda." Mr. Pruitt's voice was filled with drama. "Your word is *precipitation.*"

For the first time, the usually confident girl squirmed.

She's not sure how to spell it, Joe realized.

"Pre . . . precipitation," Amanda began. She glanced nervously at her team. "P-r-e-c-i- . . ." She hesitated a moment. "P-r-e-c-i-p-i-t-a-t-i-o-n. *Precipitation?"*

"Correct." Mr. Pruitt was very pleased. So was everyone on Team B. Amanda had done such a great job that Joe even grinned at her.

Meanwhile, back at the lunch table . . .

"I can't stand this tension any longer!" Wishbone exclaimed. He got up and stood firmly on his four paws. "It's the final showdown, and I'm not there? . . . I'm a dog of action!" He circled right. "I need to be in on the contest." He circled again. "Like the final battle Ivanhoe fights, to save the reputation and life of Rebecca."

He circled three times. He imagined himself as Ivanhoe once more, his own life in grave danger.

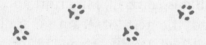

Ivanhoe is soon going to risk all that he holds dear—including his life!—yet again, for the sake of the beautiful and brave Rebecca. . . .

CHAPTER FOURTEEN

Ivanhoe lay helpless and injured in the burning castle tower. The smoke was so strong he could hardly breathe.

Suddenly, strong arms grabbed his front paws. He was lifted by two figures he could not see clearly. They carried him from the room. Ivanhoe choked and gasped for air.

The castle's stone walls crashed down as the group made good its escape. Wood floors crackled and burned, and precious wall tapestries caught on fire and burst into flames.

Once beyond the castle walls, Ivanhoe could take in gulps of fresh air. He looked at his rescuers through watery eyes. One was the black knight, dressed in his armor. The other was Gurth!

"My old friend!" Ivanhoe said happily. "And my new friend," he added, as he looked at the black knight. "I owe you my life."

"Your father is safe," Gurth told him. "So are Isaac and Rowena."

"And Rebecca?" Ivanhoe asked.

Gurth looked uneasy. "I do not want to tell you this, Ivanhoe. Sir Brian stole her away. They say he took her to Templestowe, where he lives. Isaac rode after them. He will try to ransom his daughter."

"Then I must make my way immediately to Templestowe," Ivanhoe said. "I must save Rebecca!"

"No, master," Gurth protested. "First you need to get well."

The black knight nodded in agreement.

"No. There is no time for that." Ivanhoe took one careful step forward. But his paw could not support his weight. He stumbled and almost fell onto his side. Gurth caught him just in time. His hands clutched at Ivanhoe's bloodied fur.

Ouch! Ivanhoe thought. But he made no sound. He felt as if his body had tricked him. Rebecca was in grave danger, and he could not aid in her rescue.

"Very well," he said to the black knight and to Gurth. "I shall rest in Robin Hood's camp. When I can sit atop a horse, I will go save Rebecca."

He only hoped he would not be too late. Ivanhoe told Gurth to go to Templestowe to get news of Rebecca, then return as soon as possible.

The black knight himself took Ivanhoe to Robin Hood's forest camp. When they arrived, the black knight held out his hand.

"I believe I lent you a sword," the knight said to Ivanhoe.

Ivanhoe limply raised one of his paws. "I beg your pardon, sir knight. I no longer have it."

"A pity," said the knight.

"Indeed. It was a sword fit for a king," Ivanhoe said. He added, "I wish my king would come back to England. He would heal this country's deep wounds, as Rebecca healed me."

"You're a Saxon. But you serve a Norman king," the knight said.

"I serve the English king," Ivanhoe explained. "Why is this so difficult for others to understand?"

The knight shrugged. "Few agree that we are all English. They hold on to old hatreds. Your father is one who does so."

"Do not speak ill of him," Ivanhoe warned. "Though I am cast out from my family, I am still his son."

To Ivanhoe's surprise, the black knight clapped his hands. "Worthy Ivanhoe!" he said. "You are a loyal knight—and also a loyal son. When the king returns, he shall reward you in all ways."

"I have pledged myself to his rule," Ivanhoe said. "I wish he would return. England suffers in his absence."

"I see that. And I will do all I can to bring him back."

With that, the black knight rode away.

Ivanhoe sighed. "Better hurry," he murmured.

In Robin Hood's camp, Wamba the jester cared for Ivanhoe.

Meanwhile, Rowena's wedding to Athelstane was delayed. Cedric had been hurt in the fire. He needed time for his wounds to heal.

Father, be well, Ivanhoe thought. He lay on a bed of forest leaves, lapping up broth from a wooden bowl. *Live, so that we may find peace between ourselves.*

Every day, Ivanhoe got a little stronger. Placing one paw carefully in front of the other, he slowly began to walk. His wounds began to heal. The fur he had lost grew back. He knew that soon he would have the strength to rescue Rebecca.

Then, one morning, Gurth arrived at the camp from Templestowe. He was out of breath and very worried.

"Master Ivanhoe," he said in a rush. "Isaac of York's ransom money was refused. Rebecca is to be burned at the stake tomorrow! Prince John has ruled that she is a witch."

Ivanhoe was stunned and angered. "How can he say that of her?"

"Her healing powers are like magic," Gurth pointed out. "But, worse, Sir Brian has gone mad because of his love for her. She doesn't love him, and he has lost all sense of reason."

Ivanhoe pawed the air. "I must go to her."

Gurth looked troubled. "Isaac begs you to do so. He asks you to serve as her champion. If you can beat Sir Brian, Rebecca will go free."

"Then of course I shall go," Ivanhoe said. "Only an ill-bred coward would refuse such a request. And I am a purebred Saxon, thank you very much." He raised his tail with pride.

"But, master, it will be a fight to the death," Gurth added. "And you look as if you still have not regained all your strength."

"I will fight for the cause of goodness," Ivanhoe said. "To this I dedicate myself." He placed his paw on Gurth's hand. "Do not fear, my friend. Right makes might. I shall win." Ivanhoe looked for Robin Hood and said, "Thank you for providing me with safety and shelter."

Robin Hood handed a sword to Ivanhoe. "We Englishmen must stick together."

"Indeed." Ivanhoe took the sword. Then he leaped up on his horse.

To cries of farewell from Robin and the others at the camp, Ivanhoe galloped away.

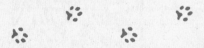

The sun was high by the time Ivanhoe reached Templestowe. He looked at the place from where he was on a nearby hill. The castle where Sir Brian lived loomed dark and grim.

The courtyard was filled with Normans. Wearing a white gown, Rebecca was tied to a stake. Dry pieces of wood were piled up and stacked around her. She looked frightened but ready to meet her fate.

Sir Brian sat on his horse. He stared at Rebecca so hard that his eyes were burning. The other knights kept their distance. Everyone was afraid of the crazed warrior. He carried no weapons.

At the stroke of noon, Ivanhoe galloped into the courtyard. He held the reins tightly in his teeth. He gripped the saddlehorn. For this mission, he did not hide behind a disguise. He wished for Rebecca— and all others present—to see his face. Ivanhoe was proud to defend the fair lady to the death.

"Ivanhoe!" Rebecca cried, as she saw him ride up toward her.

"Disinherited Saxon!" Prince John said angrily. "Why have you dared to disgrace this place with your presence?"

Ivanhoe raised his muzzle. "I am the champion of Rebecca of York. I shall defend and save her. She is innocent. I shall have my way." *Or die trying,* he added silently.

Prince John frowned angrily. "Because of her witchcraft, Sir Brian has gone mad."

"No," Ivanhoe disagreed. "She is no more a witch than you are a king."

"How dare you!" Prince John shouted. "*I* rule this land."

"No. You *bully* this land," Ivanhoe boomed. "When King Richard returns, he will make right all of your wrongs. And you will be out of a job."

"You shall die for what you have just dared to say," Prince John said. He shook his fist at Ivanhoe.

Ivanhoe raised a paw. "I don't think so," he shot back.

Ivanhoe drew his sword from his scabbard. "I will fight you in hand-to-hand combat, Sir Brian."

"So be it," Prince John said. He nodded at Sir Brian, who got off his horse and stood glassy-eyed in the courtyard. "Give him a sword," Prince John ordered a page.

Ivanhoe jumped down from his horse. He

walked toward Sir Brian with his sword tightly gripped.

Sir Brian attacked first. Ivanhoe swung at him once, twice, three times. He circled his enemy. Sir Brian ran at him. Ivanhoe ducked.

"Die, Saxon!" Sir Brian shouted. He hacked wildly with his sword, this way and that. His eyes were glazed with menace. "Die a horrible death, like Rebecca will!"

Wow! Harsh words, Ivanhoe thought. He slashed at Sir Brian's sleeve. Blood flowed from the wound. Sir Brian glared wildly at the young knight and then tried to repay the injury.

Their swords clanged, clashed, and rang for hours. The sun went down. A Norman knight brought a torch to provide light. He stood close to Rebecca, threatening her with the heat of the flame. He grinned. She swallowed hard and kept her eyes set on Ivanhoe.

I will not let you burn, Ivanhoe promised silently. *I am your champion, and I will not fail you.*

He was covered with blood. Every muscle ached. He was dog-tired. Still he fought on. Prince John and all the other nobles stared in wonder.

"Declare me the victor, and I will spare you," Sir Brian said.

"And what about Rebecca?"

"She must die," Sir Brian said. "She has cursed me with her witchcraft."

"No deal," Ivanhoe said.

They battled on. Ivanhoe had never been so tired in his life. Sweat and blood dripped from his matted fur.

I must not lose. I cannot lose, he thought.

"Will they battle all night?" asked the Norman with the torch. "I have never seen such dog-eat-dog combat!"

"'Tis a pity one will die," Prince John said. "And it had better be the Saxon."

The moon rose. The stars glittered. The night rang with sword smashing against sword.

"This cannot go on," Prince John said. "Let us burn the witch and be done with it."

Yawning, the Norman with the torch turned to Rebecca. Her eyes widened, but she did not cry out.

"Unfair!" Ivanhoe shouted. With one mighty spring, Ivanhoe flung himself at Sir Brian. In a voice filled with thunder, he let loose his battle cry: *"Whoo-cha!"*

He slammed Sir Brian to the ground and pounced on him with all four paws at once.

Panting, he held his sword at Sir Brian's throat.

"Stop! Rebecca is innocent," Sir Brian blurted out. "I only pretended to be insane because she would not love me."

"Ah-*ha!*" Ivanhoe cried. "You are busted!" He turned to Prince John. "You are a friend of death, you tyrant. Shall I kill him?"

"No, sir knight, do not slay him," Prince John said. He wiped his forehead with a shaky hand. "You have won the contest. Rebecca will be set free."

Rebecca was untied. She ran to Ivanhoe and knelt before him.

"Thank you, kind sir," she said. "You are the bravest knight in England."

"Aye, he is," a voice said softly. "And I have been a fool."

Ivanhoe turned toward the voice.

His heart caught in his throat. Cedric sat on a huge horse. The man's eyes were filled with tears.

"My father," Ivanhoe said. He took two weary steps forward, then sank to the ground.

Cedric got off his horse and ran to his son's side. "My son. My dear son. How wrong I was to cast you out. Your loyalty shames me. I am not worthy to be your father."

"Do not speak like that," Ivanhoe managed to say. "Everything I am, I learned at your knee."

Cedric put his hand tenderly on Ivanhoe's forehead. "I shall not rest until you are well."

"I will heal him," Rebecca said.

"And then you shall marry Rowena," Cedric announced.

Ivanhoe's heart swelled with joy. "She shall not marry Athelstane?"

"Bah! That chow hound?" Cedric said. "No. No man but Ivanhoe is good enough for her."

Ivanhoe closed his eyes. Tears of joy mixed with the blood and sweat on his face.

Just then, Rebecca looked up and she shouted, "Father!"

Weakly, Ivanhoe turned his head. He wagged his tail. Three more riders trotted into the courtyard toward them. In the lead was the black knight. On his left and right, Rowena and Isaac rode beautiful white horses.

Isaac jumped off his horse and crashed to the ground. Eagerly, he got to his feet and wobbled toward Rebecca.

"My daughter," he said. "I went in search of more help, in case Ivanhoe required it." He looked down at the fallen knight. "Please do not take offense. I had to do everything I could to save my daughter."

"No offense taken," Ivanhoe assured him. "You are truly a remarkable father."

"I have learned very much from him," Cedric admitted.

"I, too, have learned much," the black knight said. At that moment, he pulled off his helmet. It was King Richard!

Everyone gasped. All except Ivanhoe fell to one knee. Heads bowed low to the ground.

"You have returned!" Ivanhoe gasped. "Why did you not say so?"

"I wanted to see what my brother was up to," the king said.

"Uh-oh," Prince John muttered.

The king pointed at his brother. "And you were up to no good, John. I now strip you of all your lands and precious jewels. Everything that you had now belongs to Ivanhoe."

The king smiled at the young knight.

"You are rewarded for your knightly behavior," Richard told Ivanhoe. "Your story ends well."

Rowena got off her horse and came to stand next to Ivanhoe. He put his paw in her hand. "I'll say," he said happily.

I'd say Ivanhoe deserves all this happiness. He certainly has been tested enough in many ways to have earned what Richard has given him.

Speaking of being tested, let's go back to Oakdale. I'm sure you're as eager as I am to find out who wins the hotly contested spelling test.

CHAPTER FIFTEEN

Wishbone paced outside the school and sniffed the air with his black nose. *I hope the spelling bee ends in victory for Team A. I love happy endings, like the conclusion of* Ivanhoe. "Hoo, boy, how much suspense can a dog take in one day?"

How can I stand this excitement and tension any longer? Joe wondered.

David and Amanda were both still standing. Who would be the winner?

"*Emancipation,*" Amanda said slowly. She was obviously nervous.

The words just keep getting harder and harder, Joe thought.

"E-m-a-n-c-i-p-a-t-i-o-n. *Emancipation.*"

Her team cheered wildly. Mr. Pruitt was happy,

too. He said, "Excellent. . . . Now, David, your word is *perpendicular.*

All right! A math word, Joe thought. *Perfect choice for David.* He sat up straight, eager to see David ace it.

David flashed Joe a wide grin. *"Perpendicular.* P-e-r-p-e-n-d-i-c-u-l-a-r."

"Yes!" Mr. Pruitt shouted.

Team A cheered and applauded. Joe smiled proudly at David, who looked pleased and relieved.

"All right. Let's settle down. The spelling bee isn't over yet," Mr. Pruitt reminded the class. "Amanda, *miscellaneous.*"

Her smile was just as big as David's had been. *"Miscellaneous,"* Amanda repeated. Then, rapidly, she spelled out, "M-i-s-c-e-l-a-n-e-o-u-s."

"Oh, Amanda, I'm sorry, but that's incorrect," Mr. Pruitt said.

Amanda was shocked. Her face turned pale. She put her head down and walked to her desk and sat there, silent. Her classmates covered their faces and shook their heads. Defeat hung over them like a dark cloud.

"All right, David, can you spell the same word?" Mr. Pruitt asked.

Go, David! Joe thought.

"Miscellaneous," David said. He took in a deep breath. "M-i-s-c-e-l-l-a-n-e-o-u-s."

"Yes! That's correct. Congratulations, Team A," Mr. Pruitt said loudly. "We have a winner!"

Team A broke into wild shouts of victory. As David sat down, he said to Joe, "I can't wait to tell Sam." He smiled at Amanda. "Good contest."

The girl took a moment to calm herself before she could answer. "Yeah." She brightened up. "Good contest."

"Ha-ha! The Team A heroes are victorious!" Wishbone exclaimed after school.

The terrier, Joe, and David were on their way to Sam's house.

"When do we eat?" Wishbone asked. "Every victory calls for a feast of celebration."

The boys knocked eagerly on the door. With his excellent hearing, Wishbone detected the turning of book pages. Then he heard Sam's footsteps.

"Okay, okay! I'm coming," she called. "Just a second!"

As soon as Sam opened the door, the boys started talking.

"We won, Sam! It was awesome. The word was *miscellaneous,* and—"

"All right!" Sam cried. "Way to go!"

Wishbone stood between the two boys. "Doesn't that make you happy, Sam?" he said. "Okay, let's eat."

But Joe was staring at Sam. "Sam," he said, "you're cured."

She shrugged. "I know. The attack I got wasn't as bad as it usually is." She led the way into the living room. She sat down to hear the whole story.

"You should have seen Amanda squirm," David told Sam.

"Yeah," Joe added. "It was great."

"Oh, I wish I hadn't missed it," Sam said.

David smiled. "Well, I was squirming, too."

"You know what?" Sam said. "I would have, too."

Wishbone crept forward. "I was squirming and sweating. I think I lost two pounds." He kept creeping along, rubbing the floor with his stomach. "I was sweating worse than a glass of ice water on a hot August day. I was more nervous than a worm in a bird's nest." He collapsed.

Joe chuckled. "Look at Wishbone. I think he's pretty worn out."

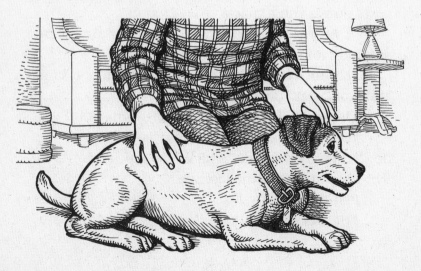

"Yeah," Sam agreed. "He looks really tired." She sat on the floor and scratched his head.

"Finally, I get a little attention around here." Wishbone's voice was drowsy and content. "Sam truly understands me."

"Sam," David said, "I'm sorry I got you sick, but I'm glad you're feeling better."

"Thanks," Sam replied brightly. "But I bet Amanda will give me a hard time about not being at the competition."

"I don't think so." Joe had a tone of mystery in his voice. "We told her that you coached David and taught him everything he knows!"

The friends laughed. All three began to pet Wishbone.

"Ha-ha!" Wishbone chuckled. "It feels great to have friends who'll help you and stand up for you . . . and also get you a snack."

As nice as the petting was, it was not producing any food for the famished victor.

"Let me repeat that last part," Wishbone said. "'And also get you a snack.'"

The three kids just kept petting him.

"Uh, please, for once, could you listen to the dog?" Wishbone said. "Snack," he repeated. "As in 'Let's high-tail it to the kitchen.'"

Pet, pet, pet.

"Helll-ooo!"

About Sir Walter Scott

Walter Scott was world-famous for the historical adventure novels that he wrote. Most of his stories were set in Scotland, where he lived his entire life.

Scott was born in 1771, in Edinburgh. His father was a lawyer. Both of Scott's parents were descendants of many famous Scots warriors. He was very proud of his heritage.

When Scott was only eighteen months old, he lost the use of his right leg. Modern historians believe he had a form of polio. He was sent to his grandfather's farm in hopes he would get well. He spent his early boyhood there. His grandparents passed the time telling him stories of days gone by.

Scott was a brilliant and curious boy. He never tired of hearing old Highlands songs, tales, legends, and folklore. He learned everything he could about the history of Scotland.

His favorite stories were about Highlanders. He loved to hear about the battles to put Bonnie Prince Charlie on the British throne in the early 1700s. Some of his own relatives died fighting for the prince.

Scott became a lawyer at the age of twenty-one. He rose high in the Scots legal system. For this reason, he wrote most of his early ballads, poems, and novels without revealing his true identity. But as his fame grew, many people figured out his secret.

Scott wrote his first historical novel, *Waverly*, in 1814. It was wildly popular. As a group, his historical novels are sometimes called "The Waverly Novels." They are his greatest legacy.

Scott loved animals almost as much as he loved Scotland. And they loved him in return. On his estate at Abbotsford, his chickens and donkeys followed him everywhere. His dog lay at his feet while he wrote.

He adored his wife and children. He spent more time writing on rainy days than he did on sunny ones. That way he would have time "saved up" to picnic with his family. His four children were also always welcome in his office.

Scott died in Scotland in 1832. His own horses carried his coffin in the funeral procession. They paused at the exact spot where he used to ride every afternoon. There he would sit quietly and study the Highlands landscape. During the funeral, the horses stood completely still for thirty minutes, as did the thousands of mourners.

About *Ivanhoe*

Sir Walter Scott is often called "the Father of Historical Fiction." In Scotland, he is also respected as the man who gave the Scots a sense of pride.

The Scotland of Scott's day was deeply divided—just as England was in *Ivanhoe*. Lowlands Scots did not trust Highlands Scots. Before Scott's stories were written, most Scots thought of themselves only as part of a family clan. But Scott's books gave them pride in their heritage. The Scots began to think of themselves as one people.

Ivanhoe was one of the first books in which low-born characters such as peasants and court jesters took the spotlight. They were shown to be intelligent and brave. This made people even prouder, for many native Scots were poor.

Ivanhoe was one of Scott's "Waverly Novels." "The Waverly Novels" were a series of exciting historical adventures. *Rob Roy* was another "Waverly Novel." These books had a wonderful effect on world opinion of Scotland. As in *Ivanhoe*, people imagined that old Scotland was filled with good, honest people.

The king was pleased with all that Scott accomplished. He made him a baronet and came to visit Scotland in 1822. King George IV was the first reigning British monarch to touch Scots soil since 1641. The king wore a traditional Highlands kilt on his visit, which made the Scots even prouder of their history.

Ivanhoe is a novel filled with noble actions and honest deeds. Scholars have noted that *Ivanhoe* is patterned after the epic poem *The Odyssey*, which Homer wrote in the ninth century. Scott loved history. He used many actual historical sites in *Ivanhoe*. The ruins of the Norman castle at Ashby-de-la-Zouche may be visited to this day.

About Nancy Holder

nancy Holder is the author of forty-one books and more than two hundred short stories. She contributed a short story to the Super Adventures of Wishbone book, *Tails of Terror*. She has also written books about Sabrina the Teenage Witch; Sabrina's cat, Salem; and Buffy the Vampire Slayer.

Nancy has been interested in history all her life. She loves British history and has been to the British Isles many times. *Ivanhoe* was a story that captured her imagination, with its knights in shining armor, burning castles, and Robin Hood.

Casa Holder has been home to several Border

collies. Border collies are sheepherding dogs that originated along the border between Scotland and England. This is the same area where Sir Walter Scott lived for most of his life.

Nancy is very interested in helping children learn to read. In her hometown of San Diego, California, she has worked on book drives for local schools. She also participates in reading fairs and readathons for literacy. The schools have made the development of reading skills their number-one priority. She's thrilled!

In her spare time, Nancy works out at the gym. So does her three-year-old daughter, Belle. The dogs, Mr. Ron and Dot, love to be taken to the dog beach. Mr. Ron likes to body-surf. After all, he lives in Southern California!

Belle and Nancy love to watch Wishbone on television. So do their two Border collies. They're all hoping he'll come for a visit. No doubt he has wonderful stories of his exciting life to share!